D1562806

INSIDE MOVES

June 1, 1978

Rico,

After all these years I
can think of all sorts of things
to write here for you, but none
of them could possibly convey
the depth of my feelings for
you. You are the best you I
can imagine, and much of
what is good in me, I got
from you.

Love, Todd

INSIDE MOVES

Todd Walton

Doubleday & Company, Inc., Garden City, New York, 1978

Library of Congress Cataloging in Publication Data

Walton, Todd.
Inside moves.

I.   Title.
PZ4.W2416In [PS3573.A474]   813'.5'4
ISBN: 0-385-13553-x
Library of Congress Catalog Card Number 77–12893

Portions of this work appeared in a slightly different form in *Gallery* Magazine.

FOR MY BROTHER STEVE

My name is Roary and I'm the kind of person that scares people just looking like I do. I'm the kind of person people see coming and lots of times they'll cross the street rather than walk by me, or if they do walk by me it's quick and nervous, like they'd walk by a dog they weren't sure of. I don't blame them at all because I am pretty gross-looking and I walk funny because I'm a cripple.

I got hurt in Vietnam. This land mine blew a hole in my upper back and destroyed some vertebrae and part of my spinal cord and part of my brain. I was paralyzed for about a year. Then one day I was talking to this guy Schulz, who was just an orderly, and I told him I felt okay, that I was pretty sure I could walk and use my arms. Next thing I know, this psychiatrist is there telling me that I'll just have to accept the fact that I'm gonna be paralyzed for life. He was trying to help me face reality, which I suppose was his job, but since I *knew* I could walk he just irritated me. Sometimes you just know something, no matter what anybody else tells you.

So I told him, "Really, Doctor, I can walk." He's a young guy, luckily, so he still has some energy and curiosity. He goes off to talk to a surgeon to find out if I can be disconnected from the bed and the tubes they had going into me. He wanted to let me try to move so I'd know I couldn't, which he figured would help me accept my paralysis. So the surgeon comes back with the psychiatrist and a couple orderlies and a couple nurses and some patients come in too. It was a big event. I could write a whole book on that hospital, but they've already written so many like it, there wouldn't be much point.

The surgeon says go ahead, unhook him. The nurses pull my tubes and then very dramatically this one nurse throws back the covers and there I am in my crummy, piss-stained bedclothes. Nobody's changed me in over a week. Like I said, I could write a book about that place, but don't worry, I'm not going to. It wouldn't be worth the trouble.

Anyway, after the surgeon says what a disgraceful situation it is, me not being changed and my tubes not functioning properly, and the nurses and orderlies get done passing the buck to some boy who works the graveyard shift, I swing my legs off the bed, push off with my hands and stand up for a few seconds before my legs, which I haven't used in a year, give out and I sit back down on the bed.

I'd give a hundred dollars right now to have a picture of all those people staring at me.

But I can't really blame them for not changing me. What difference does it make when you think somebody's just a vegetable anyway? I was just a raspy voice coming out of a scarred-up face to them. Most of them didn't even know I had a body.

So that's why I shuffle when I walk and why my head leans to the side a little. I grew a beard and let my hair get long because that covers my scars front and back, and also my head leaning isn't so noticeable with all that hair. I guess I'm fat because when I'm lonely I tend to eat to fill in for whatever I'm lonely for. Sometimes it's a girl, sometimes I just need somebody to talk to. So I eat.

But I don't want you to get the idea this book is about me, because it isn't. It's about Jerry, but I thought I'd better say something about myself so you'd know what kind of an angle you were getting. In a way, you're getting a cripple angle, but then again I wasn't born a cripple. There's a big difference between a born cripple and somebody who gets crippled. The main difference seems to be how bitter they are. That isn't always true, but take Jerry, he was born cripple and he's the sweetest guy in the world. Me, I was born straight, played fullback in high school. Me, I'm bitter. I'm no sweetheart.

2

I hang out at a bar called Max's. Even if you live in San Francisco you probably don't know where it is, unless you're a cab driver. Or unless you live near there, and even then you might not know where it is since there isn't a sign or anything. It's on Irving about ten blocks west of the Med Center, as you're going towards the Sunset District. It's a good spot for a bar. It's close to Golden Gate Park, close to the hospital, buses stop a block down on Judah, and it's fairly residential, which is nice.

It's a mixed neighborhood too. Every kind of nationality and color you can think of lives around there. Blacks, whites, Mexicans, Chinese, Filipinos, Japanese, Samoans, Russians, Poles, Italians, Jews, medical students, nurses, old people, heroin addicts, alcoholics and crazy people. There's lots of crazy people in the area because they have so many mental health clinics.

Max's is an old square two-story building that was originally a hotel but is now just Max's bar on the ground floor and rooms for rent upstairs. From the outside Max's looks closed. The Burgie sign in the window has been dead for years and the place always looks like it hasn't been painted for at least fifty years, even though it's probably only been about five. I think it's a combination of the fog, the smog, the dirt and the cheap paint. Whatever, Max's is sort of white on the outside, with three big fogged-over windows, the middle one with the dead Burgie sign, and a faded-brown door, extra wide, that opens inward automatically when you step on the welcome mat.

On the inside Max's is kept up pretty well. The bar is on your right as you come in the door and it's a real beauty. Dark wood, polished shiny smooth with all sorts of hand-carved decorations, very ornate and old. It runs all the way to the back of the room, about forty feet, without a break in it. On the wall behind the bar there's a huge old mirror that runs all the way back too. Forty feet of glass. You can see all of Max's reflected in that mirror.

There's a lot of space between the tables at Max's. There's about fifteen round tables in the middle of the place, and then booths all along the back wall and down the side wall opposite the bar. Along the street-side wall there are four pin-ball machines, a pong game, a jukebox, and in the middle of all that a gigantic television screen, five feet square, which they only use to show ball games. There are two other televisions up behind the bar at either end, and one or both of them are on almost all the time in the evenings. Sometimes Max's is dark and cool, sometimes bright and warm. It all depends on the weather and how many lights people feel like turning on. Usually it's pretty cheerful.

I met Jerry the first time I came into Max's. I was nervous as hell going in there the first time. I'd heard about the place from a guy at the VA but I didn't know what to expect. The first thing I see is Jerry, standing by the bar talking to Max, who owned the place. I felt terrible.

He had a beautiful face, very boyish, light-brown hair, blue eyes and a terrific smile. He had a great physique and when it was hot he wore tee-shirts that showed off his arms and chest. You wouldn't think he was a cripple in a million years, until he walks. Then you see he has this very noticeable limp. But even so he still seems almost perfect. At least to me.

And then Max, who always just sits on his high stool by the

4

cash register and the phone at the end of the bar just as you come in the door. Max doesn't have any legs. He has a barrel chest and likes to wear striped shirts, stripes that go side to side and make his chest look even bigger than it is. His neck is thick and his arms are short but incredibly muscular. His hands are teeny. I noticed that right off. Teeny hands like a little boy's, except tough and calloused like a ditchdigger's. Max's face is very round and he hardly has any wrinkles. His eyes are small and dark, deeply set. His face is almost always expressionless though, blank actually. He could be forty or he could be seventy, you can't tell by his face. He's partly bald on top and some of his hair is gray and some is brown. Somebody told me once that Max was German but he almost never talks, and when he does I can't hear any accent. It seems like Max is always eating a corn-beef sandwich and sipping a beer. I've never seen him eating anything else.

So anyway, Jerry was working there. He was Max's bartender from two in the afternoon until eight at night. Jerry takes one look at me and comes right up to me and shakes my hand. "Welcome to Max's," he says, smiling at me. "My name's Jerry."

At first I wasn't sure how to act. I could see by the way he walked he was cripple too, but I hadn't gotten used to being a freak yet. It's hard at first. Hard to explain too. You suffer for a long time and then you just have to find people who know how you feel. You have to find your own kind. It's really a pain that first year. It's like being born again, only without a mother, without anything but useless memories really. Of course I'm speaking about myself. It's different for everybody.

Jerry bought me a beer and introduced me to Max. Max said hello, but he didn't smile. Max almost never smiles, but he's a good person. Smiles, I found out, don't necessarily mean much. Then Jerry introduced me to a black guy named Benny. Jerry says, "Roary, this is Benny. Take a good look at him, Roary. Whatever you do, don't ever do business with Benny. He'll kill you for five dollars." Jerry's voice is very

5

smooth. Words come easily to him. That was one of the first things I really admired about him.

Benny smiled at me. One of his upper-front teeth is solid gold and it adds a little evilness to his smile. Benny might not kill you for *five* bucks but he'd kill you for something. He's so skinny I never can believe it when I look at his waist. His waist must be eighteen inches. He wears flashy suits, diamond rings and elevator shoes. I guess you'd say he was cool. You could tell he hated Jerry.

I couldn't see his eyes through his dark glasses. He ignored Jerry and just looked right at me. He takes off his floppy black hat, one of those oversized berets, which he likes to wear cocked to one side, and he takes a picture out of it like a magician, and shows the picture to me. It's a picture of a real pretty girl kneeling on the floor giving some guy a blow job. "Hey man," he says, "don't listen to the preacher. Interested? Fifty dollars and I'll take you to paradise."

"I don't have fifty dollars," I say.

"You will," he says, putting the picture back. "So do what the preacher says and remember me, man, remember Benny."

Lots of cripples are afraid or ashamed to go to whores, so they become alcoholics or junkies instead. Me, I eat too much and sometimes I pay for a woman, but I wouldn't ever go through a pimp. I know it doesn't really make any difference, but that's just the way I am.

Then Jerry takes me over to a table where some guys are playing poker. One of the guys, Stinky Robinson, is blind, so they play with braille cards. Stinky has curly black hair that seems extra black because he's so pale white. He's got a goatee and he always wears a black suit with a white shirt and either a red, a green or a black bowtie. Stinky is always bumping into people and then hugging them. He's about the only guy in Max's who does much touching.

So I sat down with Stinky and the guys and started playing and talking, and after a half hour they know how come I'm a cripple and I know how come they're cripples and I'm in. No bullshit about it. I'm just in.

3

Jerry's day went something like this. From two in the morning until ten in the morning he works in a cardboard box factory downtown near the Southern Pacific Station. Crummy part of town, lots of old falling-down factories and warehouses and a million bums, but the pay is good and Jerry doesn't seem to mind taking the trolley down there at two in the morning. I think the creepiest part of the trip would be getting off the N Judah on Market Street at two in the morning, waiting for the Stockton to take him the rest of the way. Market Street at 2 A.M., even with all the new street lights and fancy brick sidewalks on top of BART, is still a very creepy place to be as far as I'm concerned. It's deserted and it's not deserted. There's all sorts of psychos and drunks wandering around, but no crowds. Just here a person, there a person, and these bright balls of light that supposedly cut down on crime but really just make you feel like you're in a foreign movie.

By the time he gets off work at 10 A.M., Market Street is jammed and noisy and the drunks have all crashed out somewhere until lunchtime and you can't tell the insomniacs from anybody else.

Jerry usually walks up to Market Street from the factory because he gets stiff sitting for eight hours, then he grabs the N Judah back out to his apartment, which was just a couple blocks from Max's. He changes into his shorts and tennis shoes and runs down to Edison Park, which is connected to Edison Junior High, and he plays basketball for about three hours. Mostly black guys play there, but they all know Jerry and how good he is, so he never has any trouble.

After basketball he runs home, showers, changes clothes and then comes down and works Max's from 2 P.M. to 8 P.M., and then he goes home to his wife, Ann, and gives her all his money.

But the high point of his day has got to be the basketball. So what if he's crippled? He's one of the greatest players there ever was.

About two years before I met Jerry, he married Ann. If you just met Ann for the first time and didn't know anything about her, you'd probably think she was getting over a bad cold or something, because she looks kind of shot, but beautiful.

She's tall, good figure, great legs. But her face gives it all away. She's got pretty red-brown hair that comes down a few inches below her shoulders. Sometimes she doesn't touch it for days and it gets kind of ratty, but when it's just been brushed it's really something. But her face, which could be beautiful, her face gives it all away. She's a junky, for one thing, and a whore so she can junk it. It hurts me to say that, but that's the way it is.

She has wide green eyes, cat eyes, but the whites are bloodshot most of the time. She's got really striking high cheekbones, but they get bruised so she covers them with rouge. Nice, slightly upturned nose, makes her seem a little snobbish, which she is, and big sweet lips she paints dark red or not at all. She's pale, not very healthy. I saw her once after she lay in the sun for a couple days and she looked fantastic. She looked like a Southern California beach girl, about twenty years old. But that's rare. Usually she looks about thirty, tired, hating herself, treating Jerry like shit.

The story goes that she got to know Jerry because she used to come into Max's to pick up on some of the guys. She and Jerry got to be friends. She'd confide in him. Jerry's a magnet for people like Ann, and people like me. One night she goes

8

over to Jerry's apartment and tells him she's about to kill herself, nothing mattered to her any more, that bit. This is all secondhand, so I never have figured out why, but Jerry apparently just suddenly asks her to marry him. She's stunned of course, but then she says yes, who wouldn't? So the next night Jerry invites over a bunch of friends, mostly guys from Max's, there's a minister there, flowers and a cake, and he and Ann get married just like that.

Personally, I think he must have been temporarily out of his mind when he did that, because in no time she's screwing guys and shooting up right in Jerry's apartment. But he won't throw her out. Why? Because the guy believes in miracles.

4

About the only thing Jerry really splurged on besides Ann was pro basketball games, and I'm talking about the best seats in the house. Anytime the Golden State Warriors played at home in Oakland, Jerry was there. He took Ann whenever she wasn't all junked up, but sometimes he couldn't find her. She's be off turning a trick or buying stuff, I don't know. There were lots of times she just wasn't there, so Jerry would take me instead. I'm not sure why he liked me at first, but he did.

We'd grab the old clanky N Judah down to Market Street and then get on BART. I love BART. Lots of people don't like it. They say it's overautomated and always breaking down, but I think that's crap. It's fast and it's comfortable and it's clean. You go by escalator down into these fantastic futuristic stations and buy these little tickets that have a memory. They remember where you get on and how much you owe when you get off, according to how far you've gone. They say it's done magnetically, but it's beyond me.

We get on the train, barely get into our seats and we're whooshing under the bay, going downhill so fast your ears pop and then up and out of the ground into Oakland. It's really crazy because different counties passed different bonds to pay for their stretch of BART, so sometimes the train goes underground and then right at a county line it'll pop out of the ground and run along on an elevated track.

There's a stop right at the Oakland Sports Complex. You get off the train and right onto this long escalator that takes you up into the pavilion. I always felt like I was in another world when I'd go with Jerry to the games. Life in Max's bar is pretty primitive, really, and BART and the Sports Complex are like the future.

Then in the basketball pavilion we'd sit in these seats that were so comfortable you could fall asleep in them, and with my back that's quite a trick.

We always had to be there early, an hour before the game. Jerry had to see everything. He had to see them lower the baskets in place and watch the janitors dust-mop the court. And he liked watching the crowd coming in. A big crowd and Jerry would be happy. "The guys'll love this," he'd say. On a bad night Jerry would scowl. "Where is everybody? How do they expect the guys to want to play with no support?"

He called them the guys. He probably knew them better than they knew each other. Jerry could tell just by looking at them when they came out on the court to warm up, how well they were going to do.

"Jees," he'd say, "Duke doesn't look good tonight. Look at the bags under his eyes. He didn't get enough sleep last night. Last time he looked that bad, Boston killed us!" He always said "us" too. The guys and us.

He'd get more and more excited as the tipoff approached. He'd roll his program up, unroll it, roll it, unroll it. He'd make predictions. "We got 'em," he'd say, five minutes before tipoff. "By seven." Then with a minute to go, "Oh Christ, they're starting Cooley again, we're in trouble. Jesus, Jesus."

And when they tipped off, Jerry tipped off with them. I swear he jumped in his seat. Ran up and down the court in his seat, shot, passed, faked, scored in his seat. He would cry too, when something really great happened on the court. Some guy would do a double twist in midair, pass off to somebody else floating in for a dunk shot, the dunk would get blocked, but the guy who made the original pass would recover the ball and score anyway. Second efforts like that would just kill Jerry. It's not a sport for him, it's much more than that.

And the way he'd scream at the Warrior rookies, you wouldn't believe. It always surprised me how cruel he could be when he'd get wrapped up in a game. He'd shout at them so much sometimes he'd get hoarse. "You stupid sonofabitch!" he'd scream. "Pass off! Who do you think you are, Elgin Baylor? Pass off!"

Halftime, if we were ahead, Jerry was always nervous but happy. We'd eat our sandwiches and joke around. A few times we'd even talk about things other than basketball. Those were happy minutes, those halftimes when we were ahead. I think I felt normal, maybe even a little cocky, sitting there in our twelve-dollar seats, eating sandwiches heisted from Max's, talking about life and watching the girls go by.

If we were behind, forget the food. I'd get up and go have a few candy bars. You couldn't talk to Jerry. He'd have his pencil and pad out, drawing diagrams, tallying statistics, thinking incredibly hard, trying to win the game by concentrating, by going into the locker room in his mind and becoming the coach. The second half would tell if the guys had listened to him or not.

There was one month when the Warriors were doing really badly and I just couldn't bring myself to go with Jerry some nights. When I did go it was torture. I'd get really bad stomachaches. But when the Warriors were hot it was heaven. I didn't really care if they won or not, but Jerry did and I cared about him a lot.

So one night the Warriors are playing the Bullets. Watch out! Both teams are in first place in their own divisions, both of them have eight game winning streaks going. Ann is supposed to be in Los Angeles trying to clean up her act, staying away from her regular connections, so Jerry takes me along.

It's a great game, tied at the half. During tie halves, if we've come from behind to tie, Jerry's happy. If we've blown a big lead, it's me and the candy bars as far away as I can get. In this particular game it's been close all the way. Jerry is sweating like crazy. "The key, Roary," he says, tapping my arm with his program, "the key is Alvin Martin. If he can come off the bench and take charge, we've got it."

Alvin Martin was a rookie, about six feet five inches tall, very quick and strong, but inconsistent. One night he scored thirty-seven points and won the game with a last-second jump shot. Another night he missed eight or nine shots in a row and threw the ball game away with bad passes. Jerry loved Alvin, identified with him and depended on him. I guess if Jerry had anybody on the team he pretended to be, it was Alvin Martin.

The game went down to the wire. The Bullets were up by one with twenty-five seconds left to play. Alvin Martin had been sensational coming off the bench. The ball comes into him and he puts a fabulous fake on this man and is all alone from fifteen feet out. Then he freezes. It was like he didn't know what to do. Jerry was on his feet screaming, "Shoot the ball, you idiot!" But Alvin was in a daze or something. He comes out of it and starts to shoot, but too late, the Bullets' big center is there and blocks the shot, the Bullets win by one.

Jerry is beside himself. I've seen him mad before but never like this. His face is beet-red and he's grinding his teeth.

"That stupid fool," he says. And then he tells me he's going to the locker room and give Alvin Martin hell.

"Aw Jerry," I said, "he's a rookie. He panicked. Give him a break."

But Jerry wouldn't listen. He's incensed. So I follow him down on the court and we go into the hallway off the main floor that leads to the locker room. The place is crowded with people, mostly kids, trying to get autographs. Alvin Martin is standing there, sweat pouring off of him, surrounded by reporters.

"What happened, Al?" somebody asks.

"I got a muscle cramp," says Alvin.

"See," I say to Jerry. "See, he had a muscle cramp. Let's get outta here."

"Bullshit!" says Jerry. He says it loud and pushes right through the crowd of reporters until he's right beside Alvin. Jerry is about five foot nine and Alvin towers above him. "You didn't have any goddamn muscle cramp," says Jerry, "you panicked. Can't you admit that? Why do you have to lie?"

"Hey, who let that guy in?" somebody says. I start looking around for policemen. I hate being hassled.

"That's okay," said Alvin, smiling sort of sadly at Jerry.

"Thanks," said Jerry, still pissed off. "You gotta realize, Alvin, that panic is dumb. How many thousands of times have you made that shot? Just relax and you got nothing to worry about."

"Well, thank you for the advice," said Alvin, talking very cool and quietly, "but there's pressure out there, man. Lots of it. You probably wouldn't know what I'm talking about."

That was Alvin's big mistake. Jerry is a very reasonable person about most things, but not about his ability as a basketball player. "Oh I wouldn't, would I?" said Jerry, sneering up at Alvin. "Listen, I could beat you any day of the week!"

"Hey, man," said Alvin, "be cool. Don't make a fool of yourself."

"Why not?" says Jerry. "Why don't we have a game and see just how big a fool I am?"

"I'm kinda busy," says Alvin, trying to work his way out of the crowd to the dressing room.

"Tomorrow at ten-thirty," says Jerry. "Here. What do you say?"

"Oh, man," says Alvin, "don't bother me."

"If you've got balls, you'll be here," says Jerry, pointing at Alvin angrily.

Alvin disappeared into the locker room without saying anything more. The reporters were looking at Jerry like he was from Mars. But Jerry wasn't embarrassed at all. He was ready to give an interview if anybody had been interested.

Then we got on BART and whooshed on home. Everybody was talking about the game, but Jerry didn't say a word. He just stared down at his hands with a half-smile on his face. As fast as that train is, it was a slow ride that night.

We got to Max's about midnight. It's a very clear night, cold, a nice wind coming in from the sea. My neck is aching and I offer to buy Jerry a beer. "No, thanks," he says. "Gotta try and get some sleep."

"Well, thanks for the game, Jerry," I say, heading for the door.

"Yeah, sure, Roary. Hey, Roary," he says, trying to sound casual, "would you mind coming with me tomorrow, to Oakland? I don't like going all that way by myself."

"Maybe he won't even show up," I said.

"He'll show up," said Jerry, shrugging. "And if he doesn't we can go to the zoo or something. But he'll show up. Whatdaya say?"

I wanted to ask him, Why me, Jerry? What do you want me to go along for? Why not one of the guys you play basketball with? But I couldn't. "Okay," I said, "I'll go, and if he doesn't show up, no big deal."

5

That night at Max's I told the guys what Jerry had done. Louie Lum, a big handsome black guy with no arms everybody calls Wings, started laughing. "Shit, we watched that game on television. That Alvin Martin cat is black silk, now that's a fact, not to mention he be a tall sonofabitch. How in hell Jerry gonna play with him? He gonna blindfold him? I mean it's one thing to go on down to the park and play pickup ball, and something altogether different when you get out there against the best."

We ran the subject into the ground in about five minutes. There wasn't a whole lot to say. Stinky Robinson was the only guy who thought Jerry had a chance, and that's just because he worships the guy. He bet everybody a quarter that Jerry would win. They gave him ten-to-one odds.

I was walking home slow after Max's closed and just for the hell of it I went by Jerry's apartment building. He lived in an orange four-story building, pretty plastic-looking, but fairly nice and inexpensive. It always surprises me how many lights are on late at night. I wouldn't be surprised if half the people in San Francisco are up at 2 A.M., which I guess is how those markets can stay open twenty-four hours a day. Anyway, all Jerry's lights were on, so I went up. I'd never go up there if Ann was home, but I knew she was in Los Angeles. She hates me. She hates all cripples, but she really hates me. But I don't hate her. In fact, some of the time I actually like her. But she's crazy. One day nice, the next day a witch. It's the junk partly, and partly because she knows what a rotten mess her life has been. But there really is something about me that touches her off. Maybe it's because Jerry likes me, but I don't think so. I have the feeling I remind her of someone or something from the past.

So I go on up and Jerry is reading. He's a little surprised to see me, I think. It's funny but sometimes I think I look like I did before I got hurt, and I forget how I startle people now. I still dream about myself with no beard and a good back, playing football at the beach and drinking beer, resting my head on some girl's belly. I was stationed in Southern California for a while before we went to Nam. I was learning how to surf and there were girls at the beach that were just so beautiful it kills me to think that *they* chased after me. It really is like I died and was born again another person, with someone else's memory.

"Come on in," says Jerry. "I was just gonna make some coffee."

"Shouldn't you get some rest?" I ask.

"Shit, Roary," he says, "I'm so nervous there's no way I could sleep."

"What if he doesn't show up?" I ask.

"He'll show up or I'll track him down and harass him until he does show up."

He went into the kitchen to get the coffee and I sat down on the couch and stared at the blank TV screen. Jerry watched games on TV, and Ann watched the soap operas and the comedies. When it wasn't basketball season, Jerry never watched TV. Ann watched it all the time unless she was on a self-improvement kick.

You could always tell when Ann was on a self-improvement kick. First thing she'd do is put her hair in braids and start wearing glasses. Then she'd go to the library, get a stack of books and start reading. Jerry said she'd put the TV in the closet and start doing yoga every day. She'd come by Max's and help Jerry tend bar. It was an incredible transformation, but it was always so sad when she'd go back to being the other Ann. The longest improvement kick I was around for was almost three weeks. I really thought she was gonna make it that time.

Jerry had me over for dinner a couple times. That's when I

really got to hear Ann talk. I'd never go up there without an invitation when Ann was around. But she was really nice to me when I went over there for dinner. She wanted to know all about my interactions with the Vietnamese, what I knew about their social structure. She finished two years of college, majored in anthropology.

I tried to think of everything I could, but mostly when I was in Vietnam I was afraid of the people there. Little kids walked around with hand grenades, the women had knives hidden under their blouses. They hated us. What was there to know about their social structure? Sergeant says go in there and burn up the village. You walk in, see the huts spread around, a few old dogs and pigs, maybe a lost kid wandering around crying. You pick up the kid, swat at the mosquitoes, wipe the sweat out of your eyes, shoo the dogs and the pigs away, check the houses for people, and then you torch the place. You don't dare question why you're doing it, and you sure as hell don't think about social structure.

The only real interaction was with the whores, and for me they screwed like robots. Scared me how mechanical they were. They were so beautiful too, so delicate-looking, but you could just feel their hatred. There was like a rod of steel running the length of their bodies, and you just knew you couldn't ever touch them really. They didn't care for tenderness, they couldn't even recognize it they hated me so much. I eventually stopped going. I'd rather jack off than make love to a robot.

Jerry comes back in with the coffee and we sit there not talking for a while. Jerry is about the only guy I feel comfortable with not talking. I don't know why that's such a rare thing, but it is.

Jerry has a big knot of fiber and muscle and other crap about the size of a softball in his right hip. So his right leg is about two inches shorter than his left leg and every time he puts weight on his right leg it hurts. Must hurt bad because Jerry winces sometimes, and he's not the type of person to make a big deal about pain. No cripple does, because that's like making a big deal out of breathing or pissing. It's a fact of life.

"Hey Jerry," I say, "you know, I don't think Alvin Martin knows about your leg."

"So what?" says Jerry. I can hear that tone in his voice that means he's ready to scream at me.

"Don't be an asshole, Jerry. Don't give me, 'So what?'" I tell him. "He wouldn't even consider playing you if he knew you were a cripple. Would you play against me?"

"But he doesn't know," said Jerry, "so he'll probably show up and then he'll have to play me."

"If he doesn't, he doesn't. Who cares?" I'm trying to reduce the importance of the whole thing because I think if Alvin really played hard, Jerry would be lucky to make a basket against him.

"*I* care," said Jerry, his eyes burning into mine. "You know sometimes you get a feeling about something. It doesn't matter what anybody tells you, you just know you can do it. That's how I feel right now. I know I can beat him. You know what I mean, Roary?"

I said I knew what he meant, but I still didn't believe it.

6

Jerry was born in Los Angeles in 1950. His father was a plumber and his mother was a very religious Catholic. There were seven kids in the family, Jerry was the youngest. Jerry's father died when Jerry was nine, and from what little Jerry has told me, he didn't know his father very well. Jerry's oldest brother, William, who was twenty years older than Jerry, pretty much raised him. He's the one that got Jerry started with basketball. The way Jerry tells it, William was married and had a few kids of his own, but he sort of took it upon himself to take care of Jerry. But at the same time he had a lover who he liked to be with on weekends. So while everybody thought he was spending time with Jerry, he was really just leaving Jerry at a park with a basketball while he went off to spend the day with his girlfriend.

Jerry's mother is still alive, but apparently she's so religious now you can't really talk to her about much. When Jerry moved to San Francisco she told him she was disowning him for leaving her. She said he was forsaking her for the devil. Jerry said he was forsaking her for his sanity. All her other kids stayed in Los Angeles. William sells insurance and another brother is a lawyer. A couple of the kids died, one in a car wreck, one of cancer. I don't know the details. I don't even know if Jerry knows the details. He left home when he was sixteen and moved right to San Francisco. He had a cousin up here he liked pretty well. That was like ten or eleven years ago. He doesn't talk about his past very much, which is good, I think. Somehow he's gotten his past *into* the past, where it belongs.

I grew up in Worsley, Missouri. It's really a pretty town with a river running right through the middle of it. I mainly remember the humid spring days when you practically choked on the pollen in the air. And the summers when you sweated from morning until the sun went down, and on into the night in July and August. I sometimes long for those hot humid days.

I remember these two girls, Tanny and Shilah were their nicknames. I watched them grow up and I guess they watched me grow up. They were best friends all their lives. I wasn't really good friends with them, but looking back I think about them more than anything. They used to watch us play football and I remember showing off for them. Tanny was tall and thin, and Shilah was shorter but with more curves. People used to say they were lesbians, because they were inseparable. But Tanny married some guy she met at college and Shilah got married to a local guy, if that proves anything.

I remember one day I sat on the front lawn in front of my house talking to Shilah about life, about how you could look into the coals of a fire and see eternity. She was full of the same bullshit I was. It was wonderful, really. I finally told her that people thought she and Tanny were queers. I said I didn't give a damn what they were because I respected them as people. Actually I *did* give a damn but it sounded so mature of me to say I didn't, that's what I said. Shilah gave me a big hug and a very meaningful look which I pretended to understand, but to this day I'm not sure what it meant.

And I danced half the night with Tanny at the senior prom. I wanted to take her down to the river and make love with her, but her father was a chaperone and took her home before we could sneak out together. We'd been kissing and she let her hand down between us and rubbed my cock. I don't know if her father saw that, but I know he saw us kissing. I tried to take her out a few days later but she was always busy, or so she said. She got engaged a couple weeks later.

That summer after high school everybody was getting laid, looking for wives and husbands. It's an old-fashioned place. There wasn't much choice or time. One day you're a kid, the next day you're a man. Out here people grow up at all different times. Back there it was the summer after high school. We called it the Pope's Line of Demarcation.

I joined the Army at the end of that summer. I probably would have been drafted anyway but there was no one there for me, so why wait? My parents had five other kids younger than me to take care of, so I decided to just get out while I had the chance. It never occurred to me that I could just leave. I had to join the goddamn Army.

My dad was a carpenter. He was a Bible reader, we were Methodists, and when he had some spare time he loved to fish and read the Bible at the same time. He didn't have much of a sense of humor, though. He was always working too hard. My mother was the funny one, sitting in the kitchen or cutting flowers in the garden. It didn't matter where she was, she'd gossip at the drop of a hat and turn every little story into a comedy routine. I was always trying to come up with shocking little stories about my friends because she got such a thrill out of it. She was very fat and when she laughed her cheeks got so red it was really something.

I didn't want to go back there after I got out of the hospital. They flew out to see me once but what could they do? They didn't have any money. Dad could only take a couple days off work and they couldn't leave the kids alone for long. And I could tell just by looking at them and the way they looked at me, that I couldn't go home.

Mom still writes me, little notes on smelly blue stationery. She tells me what the kids are doing. She always says, "Dad's working hard and thinks of you often." I wonder if she knows she puts that in every letter. I wonder if she struggles through every letter she writes to me. I imagine she does. I don't write home much, maybe twice a year. I like to give the kids each ten dollars for Christmas. I want them to remember me as a giving person. Except for my brother Skip, none of the kids have seen me since I changed. I don't want them to, either.

7

So nine-thirty the next morning, Saturday, I go over to Jerry's for breakfast, but he doesn't have anything because he's too nervous. We trolley down to BART and ride over to Oakland again. It's a much different crowd riding BART on weekends.

Lots of families, tourists, more people together, not so many lonely-looking people. I guess maybe that's what weekends are for.

We got off at the Sports Complex and go up the escalator to the pavilion entrance. Jerry is wearing brown slacks and a nice shirt, carrying his basketball clothes in a paper bag. He seems very small to me that morning and I realize for the first time that I'm just as tall as he is. It amazes me I never noticed it before.

Jerry has been very calm all the way over, almost reverent. I feel terrible. I need a bath and I'm starting to feel really ugly, like maybe my presence will somehow ruin Jerry's chances. I'm wearing my usual baggy gray pants, tee-shirt and Salvation Army imitation tweed sports jacket. "Maybe I shouldn't come," I say right before we go into the pavilion. Suddenly I wished my hair wasn't so long.

"Please, Roary, I can't do this alone," he says.

So we go in. Jerry smiles at me when the door opens. Somebody left the door unlocked and Jerry assumes Alvin Martin left it open for him. And sure enough, there's Alvin, way down below us, popping in jump shots from twenty feet out. The ball echoes in the empty pavilion when it bounces. It's weird being there with no other people around. I feel like I'm trespassing. The place seems twenty times bigger when it's empty and quiet. We came in near the top of the pavilion, so we have a long walk down to the court. Alvin gets bigger and bigger as we get closer. By the time we're down on the court I can't believe he hasn't grown six inches overnight.

Alvin looks over at us briefly and then continues warming up. Again he didn't really get a good look at how Jerry walks. Jerry sits down on the bench and starts changing into his shorts and tennis shoes. I sit down on the bench beside him and wait. I try not to look at Alvin warming up but I can't help myself. He's incredibly beautiful to me. He's so tall and muscly, so shiny black. He moves flawlessly, like Wings said, he's as smooth as silk. He can leap three feet straight up in

22

the air, shoot the ball and land without making hardly a sound. I can't help but stare at him.

Jerry finishes tying his shoes and walks out on the court. Alvin turns and sees him walking, sees his weird right leg. "You hurt yourself?" asks Alvin, casually.

"No," says Jerry.

"What's wrong with your leg?" asks Alvin, wrinkling his brow.

I feel sick inside. Sick for Jerry, sick about everything. I just knew this was going to happen.

"I'm a little gimpy," says Jerry. "But don't worry about it, it won't affect the game."

"I don't want to play with a cripple," says Alvin. He's trying to be friendly, considerate even. You can hear it in his voice. He's watching out for Jerry. He doesn't want to hurt him.

"I'm not a cripple," says Jerry, his voice very stern. "I've had a gimpy leg all my life. Let's just play and see who the cripple is."

Alvin grins. "Man," he says, "I don't know what you've got against me, but you sure can talk a mean streak, you know it? You're famous, you know, at the games. We call you the Mouth. Duke thought that one up."

That really hurts Jerry. Here he's been living the delusion that he was one of the guys, that they were us, and then he finds out he's just a joke to them.

"We love you when we're winning," says Alvin, turning away and shooting a little jump shot. "We love to hear you yelling when we're hot, but man you come down on us so hard when we get behind. You got no mercy, it seems."

"Let's play," says Jerry, his voice monotone like some science-fiction computer.

"Listen, man," says Alvin, sounding a little tired, "I got nothing to prove. You wanna forget this?"

"You take it out," says Jerry, as if he didn't hear Alvin.

"Okay, man," says Alvin. "Don't you want to warm up?"

"No need," says Jerry, monotone still.

"Play to ten by ones?" says Alvin.

Jerry nods, his eyes already fixed on the ball.

They start to play. First thing Alvin does is go up in the air twenty-five feet out, which is a long way, and swishes the ball through. Then Jerry takes the ball in and lets it go from thirty feet out, which is so far out I can't believe he'd even try a shot like that. But it goes in anyway. Alvin doesn't say anything. He takes the ball in and puts a move on Jerry but suddenly the ball is gone. Jerry just swatted it away, limped after it and got it. Alvin closes in on him, enveloping Jerry like a huge shadow at the top of the key. Jerry has his back to the basket as he dribbles low and fast. Then he stops dribbling, fakes left, fakes right, then goes left and shoots left-handed, falling away from twenty feet on the right side of the key, swish.

Alvin says "Hmm" and smiles. He takes the ball in from half court and drives to the right of the key. Jerry's with him all the way, moving incredibly fast, sort of hopping and jerking along, and he swats the ball away again before Alvin can get a shot off. It's incredible.

Jerry has the ball again straight out from the basket, maybe twenty-five feet out. Alvin is guarding him tightly, making jabs towards the ball with his long arms. Jerry dribbles further away from the basket. Alvin lets him go unguarded when he gets thirty-five feet from the hoop, which is almost half court. Jerry shoots and goddamn if the ball doesn't go in! Three to one. Jerry leads. Alvin looks puzzled, then breaks into a little laugh.

Alvin puts a great move on Jerry, leaving Jerry looking stupid at the foul line. Alvin walks the ball in for an easy layup.

Jerry takes the ball back to half court and then brings it in. Alvin leaves him alone from thirty feet again. Swish.

Alvin burns Jerry again, taking him inside and dropping a little three-foot jumper in over Jerry's shorter arms. Four to three, Jerry leads.

Jerry comes in again, Alvin on him tight. Jerry drives, goes up from fifteen feet out, right side, Alvin up with him, his hand hovering over the ball. Jerry lets it go. The ball sneaks over Alvin's fingertips and arches high, maybe twenty feet in the air and then comes falling down, hits the glass backboard and swishes right through the hoop. I've seen Jerry play down at Edison and he's always been good, but here he's taking impossible shots, ridiculous shots, but they keep going in.

"Nice shot," says Alvin. "Thought I had you smoked." Jerry doesn't respond. His eyes are glued to the ball. Alvin brings it in and guns from twenty-five. It knicks the rim slightly but goes in. Five to four, Jerry leads.

Jerry brings the ball in, Alvin pulls back, Jerry puts it in from thirty.

"Jesus," says Alvin, grinning broadly, "who are you anyway?"

Jerry says nothing, eyes on the ball. I'm tempted to shout out, That's Jerry Maxwell, pretty fucking incredible, huh? But I don't.

Alvin brings the ball in, dribbles over into a corner and goes up with it. How, I don't know, but Jerry blocks it! Alvin is stunned. He must have been bringing the ball up when Jerry hit it, because Alvin can jump miles higher than Jerry. But Jerry blocked it and then grabbed it and ran. Alvin chases Jerry out to the top of the key and shoves him a little. Jerry ignores the physical contact and goes up with a shot, sort of a fall-away, right-handed football throw shot. It caroms off the backboard and goes in perfectly.

Alvin is pissed off, but more than that, he's amazed. Jerry hasn't missed a shot and leads seven to four. Jerry lets Alvin drive past him the next time and dunk the ball. Alvin throws the ball to Jerry at half court and then runs at him to be on him tight the second he brings the ball in. Jerry drives by Alvin, makes a beautiful inside move and goes up from five feet out on the left side. Bam! Alvin blocks the shot. But Jerry retrieves the ball and drives again, tries the same twisting inside move and this time he scores.

"Gettin it down, huh?" says Alvin, breathing hard.

Jerry nods. Alvin took two shots to get his next point, then Jerry gunned in his ninth from thirty feet again. Alvin then scored on a layup and it was nine to seven Jerry.

Jerry brings the ball in, Alvin on him like glue. Jerry dribbles to the right, cuts back to the left and from twenty feet out he lets go with an underhanded shot that swishes through to win the game.

Alvin shakes his head. "That's bullshit, man," he says. "How do you expect me to play against a cripple?"

"You asshole," said Jerry, his victory smile fading fast. "You tried and you know it."

"Bullshit," said Alvin. "I coulda blocked your shots with my feet. You're a half-court showboat Charlie, that's all you are."

"You know I beat you," said Jerry, trembling. "That's all that matters to me."

"Get outta here," said Alvin sneering. "This place is for basketball players, not freaks."

"You don't mean that," said Jerry, suddenly his old benevolent self. "I know you don't, Al. I've just had more experience than you, that's all."

"Get outta here!" shouted Alvin, slamming the ball down on the court. "You aren't supposed to be in here anyway."

"We're going," I said, standing up and gathering up Jerry's clothes.

"And take Igor with you," said Alvin, shaking his head in disgust.

Jerry sneered at him. "Anytime you want a basketball lesson, come on down to Edison Park. I'm there most any lunchtime."

But Alvin didn't respond. He just walked away and didn't look back. Jerry changed his clothes and we got out of there fast. Then we went to the Oakland Zoo. It was a gorgeous sunny day. The girls were out in their spring outfits, lots of lovely skin on display, but Jerry hardly saw any of it. He just kept shaking his head and saying, "I did it, I beat him." And then he'd slap me on the back and laugh, I think a little nervously. I don't think he could really believe what had happened, which made me very important to him all of a sudden, since I was his only witness.

8

On the way home Jerry told me not to tell anyone what happened. "Tell 'em he never showed up, if anybody asks, but don't tell them I beat him. First of all, they'll never believe it, and second of all I don't want to put up with all the crap that goes along with bragging, okay?"

"Sure, Jerry," I say, a little confused, "but you did beat him. You don't have to think he let you win, because I saw it all. He was trying as hard as he could."

"I surprised him," said Jerry, his eyes narrowing. "It would be a helluva lot closer next time. Nobody's ever ready for me the first time."

He could say something like that and it wasn't bragging. It was like the astronaut saying, "And then we stepped on the moon."

We got back to Jerry's place and he asked me up for a beer. I say sure and we go up, but just when we get to his door we hear Ann screaming. Jerry flings open the door and here are two guys standing there, one of them is holding Ann's arms behind her back while the other is ripping her clothes off. The thing is, she doesn't seem to be afraid. What she screamed was, "Hey go easy there!" Like these are her clients and they just got a little out of hand.

"Get outta here," says Ann, glaring at Jerry. She's junked out good.

"Beat it," says the guy tearing her clothes.

27

Jerry is just as calm as can be. "This is my house," he says quietly, "and that's my wife you're fooling with. Whatever you paid her, I'll see you get it back. Now please get out of my house."

Jerry calls his apartment his house. When he said the word "house" it cut right into these two guys. They were scared, you could tell. I moved into the room so they could see me too. I'm good for a scare. The guy holding Ann says, "Jesus Christ" when he sees me, and lets her go.

The other guy clears his throat. "Hey, man, like she came onto us, like we didn't initiate anything."

"I know," said Jerry, still very calm, "she asked you what you liked and said she'd see that you got it, right?"

"Twenty-five bucks in advance," said the guy who had been holding her. They were both wearing fancy three-piece suits, black ties, high-heeled shoes. They had styled bleached-blond hair and they both wore dark glasses. They could have been models or pimps, low-class pimps is what they looked like, but if they were, they wouldn't be paying for this kind of shit.

Meanwhile Ann has floated over to the couch and is watching the whole scene like it's a TV show. She's got a half-smile on her face. Her breasts are hanging out of her torn dress and she looks like a rape victim. I saw women like that in Vietnam all the time. I don't know if they'd all been raped but they had that dazed, drooly smile.

"Ann?" said Jerry, very kindly, like he was talking to a child.

"Yes, honey," she said, like a demure housewife.

"Where's the money?"

"They didn't give me any money," she said. "They're motherfuckers, Jerry. They were gonna fuck me front and back." She said that soft too—demurely, that's the word—no malice, nothing.

"That ain't true," said the guy who had been tearing her clothes. He was really skinny, with a sharp nose like a parrot's beak. "She took twenty-five bucks and she better damn well cough it up." His voice was tense and high.

"Or what?" asked Jerry, so calm it sent chills through me.

"Or this," said the guy, and he whipped out a big shiny switchblade.

"Mistake," said Jerry, smiling at the guy.

The other guy pulled a knife too. I was scared out of my mind. I'm very slow and I don't have much confidence as a fighter. These guys looked pretty wimpy, but they had knives and we didn't.

"I'll give you five seconds to get out," said Jerry, almost whispering, "then me and my friend here are gonna ram those little blades down your throats."

Jerry pulled me out of the doorway and we moved over in front of Ann. They looked at us for a few seconds and then Jerry started counting. "One, two, three . . ." They were gone.

Then Jerry started crying. He just stood there weeping and Ann is sitting there grinning like an idiot and I'm standing there scared shitless. Sometimes nothing makes any sense.

Jerry stops crying and turns to Ann. "When did you get back? I thought you were gonna stay in L.A. for a while."

"I never went to L.A.," she said, smiling sweetly up at him. "I met this guy at the airport right off the plane from France. Oh Jerry, he had such incredible stuff. Oh Jerry, it was heaven."

Kill her, Jerry, is what I was thinking. Kill her or just throw her out, but don't forgive her, Jerry.

"That's nice," said Jerry, grimacing. Then he starts to cry again. "Listen, Ann," he says, "I can't handle this any more, do you understand me? I'm finished with taking care of you. I'm gonna move out. You can have the place, the TV, everything. I've paid the rent for next month. I'm leaving, do you understand?"

Ann sort of screws up her face and squints up at Jerry.

"Hey, man," she says, "I'm pretty fucked up, what are you talking about?"

"I'm leaving," said Jerry. He wasn't crying any more. His face was hardening.

"Oh Jerry," she said, reaching out for him weakly. "I'm sorry."

"It's okay," said Jerry, backing out of reach. "You're just you and I'm just me and it doesn't work. So I'm leaving."

"Don't leave, Jerry," she said. It sounded like she meant it. I could never be sure because her tone of voice changed so suddenly from one sentence to the next.

"Goodbye," said Jerry. And then he left. He just turned around and walked out the door. Didn't even pack a thing. Didn't even say come on to me. He just left her stunned on the couch and me standing there staring at her.

"Don't you leave too," she said. She was smiling at me in a crazy sort of way. "I hate being alone," she says.

I sat down beside her and she leaned her head on my shoulder and giggled a little. "You ever tried junk?" she asks me.

"They gave me a lot of morphine in the hospital," I said numbly. I felt so strange sitting there in Jerry's apartment, alone with his wife. I always wanted him to break free of her, but now that he'd done it I realized how much his place meant to me, how much just knowing that he and Ann were there together sometimes had meant to me.

"Did you like it?" she asked, her voice suddenly very sexy.

"It made the pain less," I said, fidgeting.

"Oh, it does," she said, her eyes widening, "it does." Then she slid her arms around me. "You ever balled when you were really high?"

"No," I said. I was getting nervous. Part of me wanted to get her out of her clothes and make love to her, and part of me was disgusted with her and with myself for even thinking about it. She's the wife of my best friend, she's out of her senses on junk and part of me wants to take her. What's the matter with the world when it gets like this?

"You wanna get high with me?" she says, putting her hot

30

tongue in my ear. "I just need fifty bucks and I'll take you to paradise."

Lucky for me I didn't have fifty bucks. Lucky for me, because right then I might have done it.

9

Jerry moved into a room above Max's. Max had a room upstairs too, and Blue Louis had the other. All three of the rooms have windows facing out on Irving. There's a bathroom at the end of the hall they all shared. Pretty cramped quarters if you ask me, but Jerry fixed his room up pretty nice, covered the walls with pictures of his favorite basketball players and got a few plants on the windowsill. The room was just big enough for a bed, a desk and a chair.

Ann came around every day for a couple weeks to show Jerry how she was trying to stay straight. She started going to a psychologist at one of the free clinics and she even started looking for a job. But she was real panicky. She was going through hell trying to clean herself up. She'd come into Jerry's room and literally fall down on her knees and beg him to come back to her. Jerry stayed pretty calm, told him he'd come back when and if she kicked, really kicked, and not before.

Then one night I was in Jerry's room reading his sports magazines when Ann came in. She was really frantic. Her face was drawn real tight and she looked really old and tired, but she was straight. Her hair was in braids and she was wearing jeans and a sweater. She looked almost like a college girl. I could see she was going nuts inside, like she needed something, someone to help her quick. She tried smiling at me and her voice came out all high and squeaky. "Hello, Roary," she said, flipping her braids so they rode on her back instead of hanging down in front. She was really shaky. "Is Jerry around?"

"Jerry's working a double shift at the factory," I told her. I could tell she didn't really remember propositioning me, so I wasn't embarrassed to see her and she wasn't embarrassed to see me.

"Right," she said, smiling nervously at me. She started rubbing her hands together like she was cold, but it was nice and warm in Jerry's room. "Uh, Roary?" she said, taking a deep breath and closing her eyes. "Could you lend me twenty-five dollars?"

I could tell she wanted it for junk. I had the money but I wasn't going to give it to her, so I lied. "Don't have twenty-five, Ann," I said coldly.

"Oh," she said, trying to sound cool. "Okay, no big deal." Then she broke. "Oh shit!" she whined. "I gotta fix, Roary! You don't understand! If I can just fix one more time without having to fuck somebody, I'll make it. It's not the junk, Roary, it's the whole stinking mess!" She was crying, her whole body shuddering. I wanted to hug her but I didn't dare. I believed her in a way. If she could stop being a whore long enough, maybe that part of her would die out. But then I remembered what a con she could be and I remembered how many times she'd destroyed Jerry. Maybe I should have forgotten her past but I couldn't.

"Why don't you stay here," I told her. "Wait for Jerry. If you can just hold out a little longer."

She sat down on the bed beside me, closed her eyes again and squeezed her hands together until her fingertips turned red. "Roary, please, I've been straight now for two weeks, and I'm going to make it, I am." She looked into my eyes, her lips quivering and she really looked hurt, like somebody had cut her arm off and she didn't understand why. "I know I've been terrible to Jerry and I know I've lied and cheated and all that shit, but I'm gonna kick, Roary, I am. I'm gonna be okay, but I gotta have just one more taste, you know. I gotta taper off."

I could hear her lying now. I really resented her, not just because of her lies but because I had never been and never would be a person to her. I was a blob with money maybe and that's the only reason she talked to me at all. I think right then I really hated her. I forgot the ways I loved her. I just let myself hate her and it felt good. She was more than Ann right then, she was all the people in the world that didn't see me, except to use me and then ignore me. I hated her, so I gave her the money.

She blew it completely after that. She took up with a black pimp in Oakland who kept his girls so junked up they didn't know day from night. It killed Jerry when she went off with the guy. He was hoping and praying she'd make it. He wanted to go back to her like crazy, but he just knew she had to do it without him or she'd burn him again and again forever. Still he blamed himself.

"I should have gone off into the wilderness," he'd say, getting this half-sad, half-confused look on his face. "Taken her off to some cabin in the middle of nowhere, cleaned her up. That's what I should have done."

But how could he, I'd ask him, with no money, no job? How would he make it in the wilderness?

"You can do anything you want, Roary," he'd say, more to himself than to me. "You just have to stop thinking about it and do it."

10

I was hoping Jerry would find another woman but he didn't seem interested in looking for one. He stuck to his regular routine and banked his money. With Ann gone he didn't have anyone to spend it on. He had gone through a pretty anxious time when he first moved into Max's, but he adjusted pretty quickly and seemed almost normal. The only difference seemed to be that with Ann gone he didn't have a whole lot motivating him.

"What are you gonna do with all your money, Jerry?" I'd ask him. "Why the hell don't you spend it?"

"I don't know," he'd say. "Maybe I'll buy a house. I don't know."

He really didn't know. He'd set up his life to support somebody else's addiction. Jerry's addiction didn't cost much at all. I think for a long time he just didn't think about the money because it didn't mean anything to him. There was nothing he could think of that the money would help him get. Now me, I would have eaten out every night, kept myself well stocked with doughnuts and ice cream, traveled some and just had a hell of a time.

Then along about March the pro basketball teams were finishing up an elimination contest among all the players to see who was the best one-on-one player in the league. They'd show the matches on TV during halftimes of the regular games. It was coming down to the last few matches and it began to be pretty clear that the man to beat was Alvin Martin. The winner would get a check for twelve thousand dollars. I asked Jerry about it one afternoon when we were walking back from the park.

I used to go down and watch Jerry play, especially when the weather was nice. It was springtime, the butterflies were hatching out all over the place, and so were the sundresses and halter tops. That's one thing I love about San Francisco. Spring runs from February to June some years.

"Jesus, Jerry," I say, taking my eyes off the girls for a minute, "what if he wins? How will that make you feel?"

"Why should it make me feel like anything?" said Jerry. "Those games don't mean a damn thing."

But he was glued to the set in Max's the night Alvin Martin went against Spence Rickley, the six ten center for De-

34

troit, in the finals. Martin was superb, didn't miss a basket and easily beat the taller Rickley.

"And you wanted to play *him?*" said Bert. Bert's a great guy but he's not a cripple, so people give him a pretty hard time. He works behind the bar at Max's from 8 P.M. to 2 A.M. Bert's built like a wrestler. He's tall and thick, with huge arms. He's got an Irish face, crooked teeth, green eyes, and he wears a light-brown toupe that looks like real hair unless you look real closely at it.

"Yeah," said Jerry, faking a yawn, "I was gonna play him but he didn't show up."

"Lucky for you," said Bert, raising a bushy eyebrow. "He might have come down out of the sky one time and squished you."

I caught Jerry's eye and tried to wink at him, but when I try to wink I usually end up making a strange face. Jerry cracked up laughing.

Then they showed Alvin Martin getting his twelve thousand dollars on top of his salary, something like two hundred thousand dollars a year. But he didn't look at all happy to be getting the money. In fact, he looked a little disturbed. "What are you gonna do with all that money?" the sports announcer asked Alvin.

"I'd like to give it to some worthy cause," said Alvin, fidgeting. "Maybe to the YMCA or something.

"Give it to me!" shouted Wings, jumping up from the card game and dancing around wildly for a second. Wings has got a perfect body except he doesn't have any arms. He's tall, no flab on him, light brown and he's completely bald, gets his head shaved every Monday. "Shit, give it to me!" he shouts again. Then he grins and bats his eyeglashes at the television screen like a fag and says in a high girlish voice, "Pleez, Alvin, you can give it to my worthy cause anytime you want."

Everybody laughed at that and Bert decided for some reason that was cause for drinks on the house. Max was eating his corn-beef sandwich and didn't blink an eye when Bert started pouring the free drinks.

Jerry went up to his room after a while and I tagged along. "Jesus, Jerry," I said like a dolt, "that money could be yours."

"Horseshit," said Jerry, flopping down on his bed. "Why the fuck do I keep kidding myself, Roary? I'm a goddamn gimp, getting old fast. Why do I keep dreaming about being a pro? I'm insane, that's what I think. I actually wake up in the morning sometimes thinking I've been miraculously cured during the night. I'm just as crazy as Ann ever was."

"Hey, Jerry," I said, trying to be therapeutic, "look at it this way, maybe you will be cured someday. Shit, they said I'd never walk and I'm walking. In fact, just the other day I was in the hospital getting my neck looked at and I heard this one doctor saying they're working on artificial vertebrae that could revolutionize backs. They're figuring out all kinds of crap these days. You just can't be sure of *what* might happen."

"You're right," he says, looking up at me. Then he starts to laugh. "Maybe along with fixing my leg they'll add ten inches to my height."

"Yeah," I said, "and turn you black."

"Yeah," he said, laughing harder, "with springs in my legs!"

We ran that joke into the ground after a while and then we quieted down and both of us started reading sports magazines. Every once in a while Jerry would read me something and every once in a while I'd read him something. We used to do that all the time, looking for things that would amaze the other person.

11

By April, Jerry had almost four thousand dollars saved up. After work one night he asked me to come to his room, he had something he needed to talk about. I go in and sit on his bed and he sits in his chair by his desk and looks at me very seriously. "Roary," he says, "you remember when you asked me what I was going to do with all my money?"

"Yeah," I say, "you didn't know."

"Well, I know now," he says, smiling mysteriously.

"Oh yeah?" I said.

"You remember telling me about that doctor talking about vertebraes and stuff?" he says, getting more and more excited.

"Yeah," I said, "what about him?"

"Well, I started thinking about what's wrong with me and that maybe they'd figured out something new that could help me. So I called the Med Center and talked to this doctor and told him what was wrong with me, or what I think is wrong with me, and the guy got all excited and told me that I definitely should see a specialist as soon as possible. And so I made an appointment. And I was wondering if you'd come with me."

He's always asking me to come with him. I don't quite get it. He seems so confident all the time and then he needs me to go with him. I don't mind it, in fact I appreciate it, but I don't get it. "How come you want me to come with you?"

"Well, you've had experience with doctors, Roary," he says, "and besides I trust you and I like having somebody I can trust with me when I go places." For some reason he won't look right at me when he says this.

Then I suddenly realize Jerry never goes to a basketball

game alone either. One night when Ann was gone and I couldn't go, Jerry almost went nuts trying to find somebody to go with him. I think he finally took Stinky Robinson. "Okay," I say, "when are you going?"

"Saturday," he says. "Now you gotta promise not to tell anybody about this, okay?"

"Okay," I say.

"Saturday morning," he says, obviously very nervous. "Thanks, Roary, thanks a lot."

So on Saturday morning we go to this fancy clinic near the Med Center and sit in a very plush waiting room. Jerry is flipping through *Sports Illustrated* and I'm trying to figure out what all the letters after the doctors' names stand for. I know M.D. but these guys have got three or four others tacked on too. This one visit is going to cost Jerry over a hundred dollars. The waiting room starts to fill up with old ladies wearing mink coats and fat men with three-hundred-dollar suits on. I can see why Jerry wanted company.

The nurse, who just happens to look like a movie star, comes out and calls Jerry's name. Jerry gets up and I stay sitting down. "You come too," says Jerry, whispering to me.

"Naw," I say, "they don't want me in there."

"Can he come along?" Jerry quietly asks the nurse so no one else can hear.

"If you'd like him to," she says, smiling pleasantly.

"I would," said Jerry, reddening a little. "Thank you."

So I get up and follow after Jerry and the nurse. She leads us down a long carpeted hallway to a big room with a fancy examining table in the middle of it. There's nothing else in the room except a giant x-ray screen on one wall and a couple diplomas in very fancy frames. She gives Jerry a paper gown to change into and then leaves us alone. I read the diplomas. Dr. Carlton is a surgeon. The Air Force paid for his medical school.

"He looks qualified," I say, to kind of reassure Jerry.

"Yeah," says Jerry, "for a hundred dollars he better be."

"Where'd you get his name?" I ask.

"He consults for the Warriors," said Jerry. "I read it in one of the programs."

Somehow that embarrasses me. It makes me feel like Jerry is really a dumb kid. But then again, why shouldn't he have the same surgeon a pro basketball player has?

Dr. Carlton comes in. He has a great tan, like he just came back from Hawaii, and he seems very healthy. I got the feeling he played tennis every day with other doctors and maybe lawyers. For some reason I liked him right off the bat. He says hello to me and then turns to Jerry. "I'd rather carry out this examination in private, Mr. Maxwell."

"I'll leave," I say, starting to go.

"Could he please stay?" asked Jerry. His face is as white as his paper pj's. He really looked scared.

"If you wish," says Dr. Carlton. "Hell," he says, breaking into this enormous smile, "I'll examine him too, free of charge."

"No, thanks," I say. I've been examined enough, although I am kind of curious what a really big-shot doctor would say about me.

"Go on," says Jerry, his eyes widening. "Put on a robe."

"Okay," I mumble. I notice Jerry is smiling now with color in his face. I wonder if Dr. Carlton ever dabbled in psychology.

So he examines Jerry's hip and leg, lifts it up and down, this way and that, makes it hurt, makes it not hurt, then he tells Jerry he needs to get some x-rays of the hip. Jerry says okay.

"Good," says Dr. Carlton, "while you're getting x-rayed I'll examine your friend here."

Jerry goes with a nurse and the doctor starts looking at my back. "VA job?" he asks. I nod. "What was this?" he wants to know.

39

"Shrapnel, sir, from a land mine in Vietnam."

"It's incredible you're able to move," he says, frowning. "Any . . ." He hesitates. "Anything like blackouts, loss of memory, dizziness?"

"No," I say. "They said it was a miracle, my walking again."

"Remarkable," he says, thinking for a minute, then clearing his throat. "I'm not so sure you couldn't be improved upon."

"It would cost a fortune," I said. "I don't have the money."

"The Army would pay for it. They owe you," he said. I think he was actually a little bitter about it for some reason.

"They make you go to *their* doctors," I say, getting a little angry myself.

"I was one of their doctors once," he says, smiling at me.

Like I say, I like him. He's got a certain energy about him that makes me believe in him. He tells me he knows an Army neurosurgeon in Florida that would just love to work with me. I'm confused because I like this doctor and I'm very grateful for his concern, but I know, just like I knew I could walk, that I'm as good as I'll ever be and the thought of them cutting me open again and by some fluke paralyzing me again is just more than I even want to think about. But I leave him my address anyway in case his friend wants to contact me.

Jerry comes back in smiling. He's been joking with the nurse. She obviously likes him and he's warming up to her. Jerry sure could use a few good experiences with women. The nurse gives Dr. Carlton the x-rays and he puts them on the screen for us to look at. You can see this incredible knot of junk in Jerry's hip.

After a while Dr. Carlton turns to Jerry. "And no one ever thought an operation would help?"

"I only went to a couple doctors when I was little," said Jerry. "I haven't been since I was like eight."

"My God," said Dr. Carlton, almost angrily, "don't misinterpret me, Mr. Maxwell, but didn't it ever occur to you to have yourself re-examined before now?"

Jerry smiles and shrugs. "No," he says. "Should I have?"

"Well, I could be wrong," says Dr. Carlton, frowning. "But I don't think so. I think with proper surgery you could be almost as good as new."

"It would be the right length" asks Jerry, breathlessly.

"The problem isn't with your bones," says Dr. Carlton, tapping the x-ray with his pencil. "Surgery certainly wouldn't hurt. I see no reason why we shouldn't go ahead and operate, get things straightened out in a hurry."

"Well, the money," said Jerry, looking at me. "I'm not a veteran. I was born this way."

"Well now, if you're unemployed there are emergency funds . . ."

"I have two jobs," interrupted Jerry. "How much do you think it would cost? I mean about how much?"

"Well, the surgery would be a few thousand dollars, but the hospitalization, physical therapy, possible secondary operations, it might run anywhere from ten to fifteen thousand dollars, maybe more."

Jerry smiles at the doctor. "Well, I'll have that in about a year," he says confidently. "Could you do it in a year?"

"Yes," said Dr. Carlton, squinting seriously, "but the sooner the better. You appear to have some internal bleeding in there that could worsen at any time, and there's no telling the extent of the nerve damage so far. The aggravating thing is that this all might have been cleared up years ago, whereas now . . . well the sooner we go in the better, that's all I can say. I just wouldn't wait too long if I were you. Perhaps you can borrow the money."

"I don't think so," said Jerry, "but I'll be back in a year or less, okay?"

"All right," says Dr. Carlton, shaking Jerry's hand.

I say thank you too and we start getting dressed.

41

"In a year," says Jerry, dressing fast, "if I bank a thousand a month, I'll have it."

"Couldn't you borrow it?" I ask him, wanting him to get the operation right away.

"From who?" he says sarcastically. "You?"

12

That afternoon I made a decision. I decided I was going to help Jerry get that money. So on Monday I went down to the unemployment office, which is another book in itself. I filled out an application and then waited for about two hours in the most uncomfortable chair in the world and finally, after I'd read every poster on the walls six times and made up stories about every one of the poor suckers waiting with me, this woman calls my name.

I follow her to her desk and she has me sit down in a very comfortable chair. I told her they should do something about the terrible chairs they have for people to wait in. She smiles at me and laughs. I think she thinks I'm joking. She's actually quite attractive. Your basic peppy blonde, with a very nice figure, and you can tell most of the men who work there can't keep their eyes off her. Personally, I think she wears too much makeup and from the way her forehead is wrinkled I'd say she worries too much, about what I don't know.

"Now," she says, smiling at me like she's trying to sell me something. "You entered the Army at nineteen, were discharged at twenty-one, you are now twenty-four. You list rudimentary carpentry as a skill. To be quite honest with you, Mr. Wilson, it looks like you could use some vocational training. Now we have pamphlets . . ."

With all that crap about hire-the-handicapped plus hire-the-veteran, you'd think I could get a job. Maybe if I was a black woman too, and blind, maybe then they'd give me a job.

So I start thinking, What can I do to make money? I don't know how to do anything specialized, I can't do heavy physical labor, I'm too ugly to be a salesman. Then it hits me. Start my own business.

When I was in high school my friend Rudolph Becker and I would borrow my dad's routers and make really fancy wooden signs. Rudolph would draw the design on the wood and I'd do most of the routing. I don't know whatever happened to Rudolph. I think he went to law school. I should write my mother about him because we were really good friends. We made pretty good money even back then. So I get the idea, why not buy a router, get a GI Loan to lease a little store for a year and set up a wooden sign business. All I'd really have to find is someone who can draw different kinds of letters pretty well.

A few days later I go to the bank. I've bathed and put on a slightly newer sports jacket and brushed my hair back. I still look like the werewolf but I'm a little more presentable than usual. I see this guy and tell him my idea. I figure I'll need about three thousand dollars. He gets out some pamphlets and starts figuring things out on a calculator. He's very efficient and friendly. He reminds me of some actor I've seen before. The kind of actor that's so handsome and smooth, mostly smooth, that the women just climb in bed with him when he looks at them. That always kills me how they don't even have to say a word and the gorgeous woman just climbs into bed with them. I know it's not real but they show it as real and it gets to me every time. He could be Scandinavian, I guess, maybe that's why he looks so smooth.

He says I'm a very good risk because I'm 95 per cent disabled. That means I get a pretty good check every month and I don't have much to spend it on, though I always seem to be broke. I pay a hundred dollars a month for food roughly and my rent is two hundred and thirty-five dollars a month, so I guess the rest goes for eating out, beer and things. Then the guy checks my account and sees I've never overdrawn, in fact, it turns out I've got nine dollars in there I didn't even know about. So he gives me the loan.

Then I go home. I live in an old brick apartment building on Fourth Avenue, one block up from Irving. Three rooms, quiet place, about eight blocks from Max's, about three blocks from the Med Center, and about four blocks from Golden Gate Park. It's no big deal but I like it. I've got a waterbed, which is the only kind of bed I can sleep comfortably on, and I'm on the ground floor, so there's only a few steps to deal with. I can handle steps but they aren't my favorite pastime.

After a good nap, which I needed because I get exhausted when I have to talk with people I don't really know, I call up Switchboard, which is an alternative information service, and I get the names of five or six artists who are looking for work.

The first one I call is only into Zen Representationalism and so I say forget it. The next one I call is a woman named Valerie. Immediately I let her know I'm a disabled veteran. You have to do that or when they see you they resent you like hell for not giving them fair warning. So I tell her my idea and she sounds excited. She sounds older and very sweet. But she says forget the store, we can work out of her garage. She's got a gigantic empty garage we can use as a workshop. I can't understand why she's being so nice to me. I start thinking maybe she's a hustler, a con. So I set up an appointment for that afternoon and then I hurry over to Max's for a few beers. I'm so nervous I can't stand still.

You have to understand why I'm so inept in situations like this. I sort of missed out on a pretty important part of growing up. I got blown up as a teenager and got let out of the hospital as an adult. I never experienced the transition. My adulthood was just sort of decreed by the passage of time. So I lack a great deal of confidence, and besides, I know I'm ugly. I know I scare people, and that doesn't help my confidence much either. So it took about all the guts I had to go to the bank and what little I had left got used up calling Valerie, which means I'm all out of confidence. So where do I go? Max's of course.

Jerry has just come on and is in great spirits. "Hey Roary," he says, "I got a raise at the box factory. Eight twenty-five an hour. It won't take me but ten months now." He winks at me and smiles. I'm thinking, How am I gonna keep from telling my best friend that I'm starting a business? I drink three or four beers and then I can't help myself.

"Hey, Jerry," I say, "I'm starting a business."

"You're kidding," he says, still lost in his own financial dreams. "That's great."

I tell him about it and he congratulates me. "I was starting to worry about you, Roary," he tells me, pouring me another beer. "You're too smart to not be out working and meeting other people."

"You too," I tell him. "You need a good woman, Jerry."

"After the you-know-what," he says. He's so happy, so confident. I guess he assumes the operation will be a success. And what if it isn't? Jerry's too trusting, I think. I'm amazed Ann never brought home some psychopath that murdered them both.

So I go over to Valerie's. She lives way up on Twin Peaks, which, if you didn't know it already, is a very fashionable part of town. I start to feel almost sick to my stomach in the cab as we get closer to her house and the neighborhood gets fancier and fancier and the houses get bigger and bigger and the view out over the city and the bay gets more and more spectacular. I start to feel slimy and monstrous. I decide I can't go see her but at least I can walk by her house and see where she lives just for the hell of it. It's a windy day, a crummy day for April.

I get out of the cab a block from her house and walk slowly

towards it. Some kids go by on skateboards and one of them says to his friend, "Hey, did you see that guy? What a weirdo!" That does wonders for my confidence. Now I'm afraid to even just walk by her house.

She's got a beautiful place, a nice old Victorian joint, painted white with black trim, big curved windows, two blossoming cherry trees in front. Plus she's got a view of the whole city that'll add two hundred dollars to your rent all by itself. Goddamnit, I'm thinking, I told her I was disabled. I should have told her I was disgusting to look at too. You don't say things like that, but those are the things that need to be said.

I'm about to turn around and walk down the hill when the front door of her house opens and this very nice-looking woman comes out smiling at me. She's maybe forty-five and she's wearing a paint-stained smock over a pair of blue jeans. She has short gray hair, nice blue eyes and she's got a Hawaiian tan like Dr. Carlton's. When she talks her voice is very clear, her pronunciation perfect. You can tell right away she's well educated. "You must be Roary," she says. Then she comes up to me and puts her arm through mine and leads me up the stairs to her house. "I'm Valerie," she says, then she laughs. "I guess you knew that."

"No," I said, "not till you told me." I'm thinking to myself, If she's a hustler trying to get my money, she sure lives in a nice house. She must be good at it.

The place is incredible on the inside. Stained-glass windows, beautiful wooden furniture, tapestries on the walls, aquariums all over the place full of tropical fish, thick Persian rugs on the floor, and she's got these two enormous Afghan hounds, Mortie and Minnie, two of the goofiest-looking slobber pusses I've ever seen. They seem to like me. Most dogs snarl when they see me. These guys are too stupid to know any better, I guess.

We go into the living room and there's tea and cookies ready for us. I can't believe the place. I feel like such an idiot.

Why do I get into these situations? I'm about to apologize and tell her I think I made a mistake when she hands me a teacup and a cookie and tells me to follow her.

"I suppose we should sit and eat," she says, "but I have to show you the workshop first." We go down a hallway full of sculptures, and then down these wide carpeted stairs into a garage which has been converted into a workshop. There's every kind of woodworking tool in the world there.

"An artist used to live here with us when my husband was still alive. This was his shop. He left when my husband died. The place hasn't been used in three years." She stopped talking, remembering her husband or the artist I guess. Then she broke out of her silence and gave me this nice but nervous smile. "What do you think? When you called this sounded like the perfect place for you."

"It's nice," I say, "but I haven't done much woodwork in the last couple years."

"Well I've *never* done any lettering," she said, laughing in this reassuring way. "So we ought to get along splendidly."

"I have three thousand dollars," I said. "I guess we can use that for wood and advertising." I didn't know what else to say.

"All right," she says, "I'll put in three thousand too. We'll go halves."

I'm amazed. I'm also a little insulted. She doesn't even know me. She doesn't even know if I can do anything.

We go back upstairs and sit down in the living room and eat the cookies and talk. I tell her about myself, about Jerry, about how little experience I have. She tells me she can tell I'm a good person. She also tells me that she's fifty-three and has been moping around for three years since her husband died and it's about time she did something with her life.

I like her. What can you know about a person in a half hour? It seems like all the people I really love, I got to love in about two minutes.

We decide to call our company Roaring Valley Signs.

47

After tea we go downstairs and she gets out a big rectangle of redwood, maybe two inches thick, three feet by four feet, and then she sets it on the worktable and we clamp it in place. Then she gets a felt pen and draws Roaring Valley Signs in really beautiful Gothic letters on it with all kinds of ivy vines, birds, flowers and squirrels covering the thing. It's really beautiful. Then I get out the big router and go to work cutting out what she's drawn.

Luckily, the guy who set up the shop had all kinds of routers, one really tiny one that I use to do the details. She leaves me alone working and goes upstairs to fix us something to eat. I can feel how wobbly I am. My arms are pretty weak. I can see it's going to take me a while to get in shape. Then a little while later she comes back down and tells me it's nine o'clock at night! I've been working five hours!

"My God," I say, "it seems like a half hour at the most."

She smiles at me and then comes and hugs me. "I'll have to learn to rout too," she says. "The drawing takes no time at all."

That was one of the happiest moments I can remember. We went upstairs and ate dinner and then I left to go tell Jerry what had happened. She wanted me to stay there overnight, but I was bursting to tell somebody what had happened.

13

The next day was one of those days that people who aren't from San Francisco but have just visited for a week almost never see. You have to be there all year round for a couple years to see a day like this. Deep-blue sky, dark blue, so dark people keep shaking their heads in disbelief and I keep expecting an article in the paper to explain it. Flowers in bloom everywhere, fruit trees exploding white and pink, warm air pushed around by a light breeze. Perfect, in other words. It's the kind of day when I can't imagine anybody committing a crime.

I went back to Valerie's that morning and I could tell something had changed in her. She was still very nice to me, very energetic in terms of helping me, but I could tell something had changed. Maybe *she* hadn't really changed, maybe she had just realized something. I knew it had happened too fast. I knew she hadn't been seeing me, she was seeing an idea or an illusion of something she was hoping for.

Still I went ahead with the work. We planned to do five or six signs, send out invitations to prospective clients and have an open house. At lunchtime I could see she was embarrassed about something because she wouldn't look right at me. She was changing right before my eyes, pulling away. We sat down at the kitchen table and I told her she seemed somehow reluctant. I told her I'd understand if she wanted to back out. She denied she wanted to. She stared out the window at the incredible blue for a moment and then she said, "Oh, I'm just moody. You'd have to know my background before you'd understand my moods."

"So tell me your background," I said, thinking that maybe if I could get to know a little about her, it would be easier to understand when things fell apart. It seemed inevitable that they would.

She grew up in Boston, the daughter of a very wealthy banker. Her mother was from great wealth too and collected art all her life. When she was only sixteen Valerie went to Radcliffe, and after graduating from there she came to California and got a master's degree in art history at Stanford. Then she married a rich San Francisco banker who was twenty years older than she was. They went to Europe twice a year, collected art, gave fancy parties, knew dozens of famous people. She knew William Faulkner. She was always very

49

busy, very social. But when her husband died she just stopped everything, had a quiet nervous breakdown as she called it and hid in her house.

"Did you love him?" I asked her. That seemed to be the thing missing in her story. There was no mention of love or hate or any emotions, just names of people and things.

She laughed when I asked her that. She was very pretty, I thought, and very young-looking for fifty-three, so when she laughed she really looked young, except for her eyes, which were somehow wild, and she seemed a little afraid of something, not of me, maybe of being alone in the world.

"Oh," she said, "I adored my father. My psychiatrist and I decided I married a version of him. So, yes, I loved my husband, whatever he was. I certainly needed him." Then she looked down at her hands and smiled.

I was thinking, Listen, Varlerie, I'm not your father or even a version of him, or even a son you never had. I'm a very different sort of person. But I couldn't say that. Instead, I asked her if she really thought making wooden signs was going to be what she wanted to do for a while. She said yes, but she wouldn't look me straight in the eye when she said it. I probably shouldn't have put her on the spot like that, but I was getting such strong feelings of doubt from her.

I worked a little more that afternoon and then I went upstairs and found her in the living room, sitting on the couch looking through a big art book. Her dogs were lying sad-eyed and bored on the floor in front of her.

"I'm going," I said. "I'll be back tomorrow."

"What time?" she asked, looking up from the book but not getting up.

"Whenever you say," I tell her, shrugging.

"Why not come in the late afternoon," she says. "We'll work into the evening."

"Okay," I say.

I can just feel the end is coming. It's so useless pretending she still wants to do this. She really doesn't want to do this. I do because I have this other motive, getting money for Jerry. She doesn't have a motive except whether she likes it or not, whether it's the perfect thing for her, and I can tell it isn't.

That night at Max's, Jerry tells me I'm projecting my own self-doubts onto her. I tell him that's bullshit, I can tell when somebody is pulling away from me, but he insists I'm imagining most of it. So I get a pitcher of beer and go off in a corner booth and I think about it. I go over all the details and I try to look at it from her side as well as mine. I think of how warm she was the first day, how distant she was the second. How she hugged me the first day and seemed afraid to touch me the second. No, I'm not projecting.

I decide to go over there in the morning instead of waiting until the afternoon. I want to get things out in the open. I didn't sleep at all wondering about things and I hate it when I can't sleep. That's why I never drink coffee. Going over on the bus I'm really irritable. Me, the slowest person in the world, I make some crack to an old lady ahead of me who was having trouble getting on the bus. I'm not myself that morning. Everything seems sort of unsubstantial. All the buildings I see on my way over there seem to be crumbling. And on top of it all, it's not such a wonderful day like the day before. It's a San Francisco fog out special and everything seems especially dirty.

I get off the bus and start walking towards Valerie's. I'm about a block away and I see these four big moving vans parked in the street in front of her house. There must be twenty-five men working, loading the trucks with all her stuff. I can't believe it. For a minute I think maybe she's actually moving away to avoid me, but I can't believe she'd go to all that trouble. She doesn't even know me!

Now I don't know what to do. Do I go ahead and confront her while she's in the middle of making her getaway, or do I just forget about it? Then I remember she has three hundred dollars of mine that I gave her for wood we were going to order. That decided it. I walk to her house, go up the stairs and start to go in. There's a young woman standing by the front door with a clipboard checking things off as the men go out. She sees me and gasps. Then she smiles and laughs nervously.

"Oh," she says, "you must be Roary."

"Yeah," I say. "Is Valerie around?"

"I wasn't expecting you until later today," she says. She's pretty and slim, but you can tell part of her slenderness is from nervousness. You can tell she's afraid of me. She seems very rigid and her smile isn't convincing, because her forehead stays wrinkled a little.

"Where's Valerie?" I say.

"Valerie has gone to Europe," she says, raising her eyebrows. Now she's really nervous. "She flew to London this morning."

"Is she selling the place or what?" I ask. I don't know why I'm asking. What difference does it make? I feel incredibly tired. My eyes start to close.

"She's selling everything," she says. "She left some things for you in the garage."

I didn't want to go down. I just wanted to get out of there, but I thought maybe my three hundred dollars was down there. So I go down and here are all the routers lined up on a table and there's an envelope for me. I open it and there's a check for five thousand dollars and a little note.

Dear Roary,
    Sorry for the inconvenience. Please accept this money as my way of apologizing and please take the routers. I guess you were right.

                                                    Yours, Valerie

What was I right about? I sure wasn't right about how crazy she was, or how dishonest. So I take the goddamn money and the smallest router and I go back upstairs and find the young woman with the clipboard. She's in the kitchen checking off how many glasses are going into each box.

"Hey," I said, "if she asks, I took the money, if that helps her sleep any better." I said it without thinking. I felt so bitter. I guess I shouldn't have been mad but I was. I guess I would have rather had a friend than five thousand dollars.

The young woman looked terrified, like maybe she thought I was going to smash something. She talked very apologetically to me, like I was insane and she had to watch out for me. She said she was sorry Valerie didn't stay to explain things to me.

I said Valerie did explain things to me. She explained like everybody explains, by leaving or paying me off or getting what they can and getting out. Jerry is the only person who just *is* with me. I shouldn't blame people. I'm no prize.

So I figure now I've got almost nine thousand dollars. I don't need to start a business, shit, I *am* a business, a charity business. My money plus what Jerry has should be enough. But why she had to sell the house I don't understand. She couldn't have done it just because of me, that would be too crazy to even think about. Maybe I was the last straw or something.

14

When I get really confused I like to go to the movies. There's something about the dark coolness of a big old movie theater that relaxes me, and then the movies help me escape into fantasies, which I can do by myself, but the big fresh images speed things up. It helps me sort things out, which is what I needed to do after Valerie ran off. So I went to about five movies in the next couple days and didn't go back to Max's until I had decided what it all meant and what I was gonna do next. What it all meant I couldn't really tell you, but at least I felt like I had things in perspective better.

So I get over to Max's about ten-thirty at night after a double bill of French romances, and Blue Louis and Wings are leaning against the wall outside on the sidewalk, both of them looking like the world is coming to an end.

"What's the matter with you guys?" I ask, feeling sort of haughty with all my money, no matter how I got it.

"Max is gonna die," says Blue. Blue looks like a great big kid. He has a huge head, a short, perfectly round Afro, and smooth round cheeks.

"What?" I say. "I can't believe it."

"He had a heart attack just after Jerry opened up today," says Wings, barely able to talk. "Jerry's been down there at the hospital with him all day." Wings seems pretty calm, like he's trying to comfort Blue.

"Hey, Roary, do you think they'll close the place?" says Blue, shaking his head. "Do you think I'll have to move?"

"I don't know," I said, "I'll go down and talk to Jerry."

"I just know they're gonna close the place," said Blue. "I just know it." He clutches my arm and squeezes. The bastard has got two arms' worth of strength in that one arm.

"I'll talk to Jerry," I said, patting him on the shoulder and pulling away.

I grab a Judah over to the Med Center. Lucky for Max we're so close. All the way over I'm thinking about all the guys who live, actually live, for and in Max's. Me, I've gone two or three days without going there, though I like to go every day if I can. But guys like Stinky and Blue and at least a dozen other guys are waiting to go in when Jerry unlocks at two in the afternoon and they're reluctant to leave when Bert locks up at two in the morning. It's like a club and a church and a family all rolled into one. If Max's goes, life would seem pretty bleak around here.

I've been to the Med Center hundreds of times, usually just to sit around outside and watch the girls. They've got a Med School, Nursing School, Physical Therapist School, all the things I need, and it seems like the best-looking women in the world go there. So I go there, just to look of course. But that night I get lost looking for Jerry. I find Emergency all right, but then they send me to the heart-attack ward and somehow I get on the wrong elevator and I end up in Pediatrics and scare the crap out of a couple little kids who are about to get in the elevator but when they see me they back away like I'm some kind of an escaped killer.

So I finally find Jerry in the Cardiac Arrest waiting room. He's cleared off a table and is going through a pile of official-looking documents. It seems to me that's a pretty weird thing for him to be doing in a hospital, especially with Max nearby dying maybe.

"Hey Jerry," I say, out of breath, my neck aching.

"Hey, Roary," he says, hardly looking up from the papers, "I'm glad you came down."

"How's Max?" I ask.

"Oh, he's probably gonna make it," says Jerry, finally looking up at me and smiling. "He's resting now. The doctor says he thinks Max hadn't slept in several days."

"That's funny," I say, not meaning to but laughing a little anyway, "I never thought of Max having to sleep."

"Me neither," said Jerry, starting to look at the papers again. Right then I get the image of Jerry as a big businessman. He has that clean-cut, clear-eyed way about him. Even if he doesn't, he really *seems* to know what he's doing.

I sat down beside him and watched him flip through the documents. He seemed more interested in them than in me or Max or anything. I was going to tell him about the money from Valerie but before I get up the nerve he starts telling me about the documents.

"These are mortgage statements," he says. "The reason Max wasn't sleeping was probably because he knew he owed

55

so much money and he didn't have anyplace to get it from. He owes eleven thousand dollars in back payments. I'll tell you, Roary, Max's costs a lot more to run than it makes, if I'm reading Max's records right. They were bending over backwards not to foreclose but they finally had to, I guess. Max got the foreclosure letter today. That's probably what pushed him over the edge. Worried himself into a heart attack."

"What are the guys gonna do?" I ask. Really I'm wondering, What am *I* gonna do?

"Only one thing they can do," says Jerry, shrugging. "Come up with eleven thousand dollars or find another bar."

"We could buy it, Jerry," I said. It just hit me. We could buy it.

"What are you talking about?" he says, looking at me like I'm crazy.

"That's what I was gonna tell you," I say. "I got some money that I was gonna lend you for the operation. Nine thousand dollars."

Jerry's eyes widen and he swallows. "Are you kidding, Roary?" he says.

"No," I said. "I got it on me, in fact."

I get out the check from Valerie and the check from the bank and hand them to Jerry and he just holds them, looking at them for about a minute, breathing deeply. "Jesus, Roary," he says, "I've got nearly five thousand." Then he sort of goes into a trance and says in a whisper, "Now I guess I can get the operation. I can."

"Except Max's," I say, and that snaps him out of it.

"Oh, of course," he says, looking at me kind of sheepishly. "Of course, Max's."

Max's hospital bill came to almost a thousand dollars by the time he got out five days later, and so it cost me all of my nine thousand and Jerry about three thousand, and then we had to pay a lawyer to finalize the ownership transfer and we had to buy insurance and suddenly I own three fourths of Max's, Jerry owns a quarter and Max is back on his high chair by the cash register like nothing had ever happened.

We sat down with Bert, Jerry and I, and we figured out how much we'd have to raise prices and how much longer we'd have to stay open each day in order to make payments and maybe even make a little profit over their salaries. I really felt weird sitting there in Max's, my bar, listening to Bert read off wholesale beer prices and watching Jerry calculating profit per barrel and stuff like that. I mean I used to think of Max's as my bar in one way, but I still can't think of it as my bar in terms of owning it. If anybody had asked me before would I like to own Max's, I would have told them that Max's wouldn't be Max's unless Max owned it. But that turned out not to be so. Even after Jerry and I owned it, and later when Bert bought half of my share, it was still Max's. He didn't have to own it, but he did have to be there.

Maybe it's his eyes. They seem to be looking inward, so sadly. Or maybe it's because he isn't anybody's friend. He has no favorites that anybody knows about. He accepts everyone equally, it seems. Maybe that's it. You're not only allowed in Max's, you're accepted by Max.

I brought it up. I interrupted their figuring and said, "We have to have Max. It wouldn't be right without Max."

"Of course," says Jerry, slightly irritated I even brought it up.

"Absolutely," says Bert, lost in his figuring.

"Why is that?" I ask.

"It wouldn't be Max's," says Jerry. "The point is keeping it Max's."

"I know," I say, "but *how* does he do it? How does Max, this particular Max, make it Max's?"

"I know what you mean," says Jerry, thinking for a moment, chewing on his pen, "but I don't know."

"Aw, shit," says Bert, shaking his head like we're two dum-

57

mies, "it's Max's cause it's Max's, Christ. Now let's see, Budweiser we go to thirty-five cents a glass . . . that's a little glass I'm talking about."

15

We decided to stay open from 11 A.M. until 1 A.M. That way we could get in on the lunch trade. We hired a sandwichmaker, an older woman named Edith. She's tall and skinny but very strong. The older guys learned pretty quickly not to mess with Edith. She's got gray hair which she's always wearing in different ways. Sometimes in a bun, sometimes in a ponytail, sometimes she gets a permanent and looks like a housewife. You never know how Edith is going to do her hair. But her face is always the same. She doesn't wear any makeup except sometimes very pale lipstick. She has really nice features and even though she's got quite a few wrinkles her beauty still comes through. She has a very strong face. Big gray-blue eyes, a long but not too long nose, a young mouth, young lips and sometimes I think her chin may be a little small, but sometimes, depending on her hair style, it seems just right. You get the feeling from her face that Edith is a proud person, which she is.

She makes sandwiches like a machine as far as how fast she can turn them out. She worked at the Holiday Inn as a pantry maid for twenty years until they made her retire. She fits right in at Max's. She knows thousands of wisecracks, which she delivers slowly in a deep husky voice, and she knows how to make a good sandwich without it costing anybody too much.

We decided I should open up at 11 A.M. and serve drinks until Edith comes in at eleven-thirty and Jerry comes in at noon. He changed his hours at Max's to noon to six. Then he works at the box factory from seven in the evening until three in the morning, sleeps until nine or ten, and plays ball until he comes to work at Max's. He liked it better, he said, waking up to basketball.

And Max lives here for nothing. It's funny, nobody even discussed it with him. He signed all the papers making the place ours without saying a thing and just went back to his old routine. I wonder if he's inwardly relieved or happy. I wonder what he would have done if we hadn't bought the place. I guess he would have just let himself die. I don't know that but it seems likely.

I finally got to see him come from his room upstairs to his high chair by the cash register. Now I've seen him come and go hundreds of times, but that first time was really something. That's why I always had trouble imagining Max sleeping, since I'd only seen him sitting there, legless, and I couldn't imagine how he got there. I knew nobody helped him but I just never let my mind try and visualize it.

What he does is, he walks on his hands down the hall from his room to the top of the stairs. When his hands are flat on the ground his torso doesn't quite touch the ground. Once he's at the top of the stairs, he spreads his arms and holds onto the handrailing and works his way down like a gymnast. Coming down, no part of his body touches anything except his hands on the railing. Then he walks on his hands across the floor from the bottom of the stairs to the far end of the bar. There's a pole there and he climbs it, hand over hand, until he's right up to the level of the bar top, then he swings onto the bar. Then he walks on his hands down the length of the bar to his chair, which he pulls close to the bar, and then as he grips the edge of the bar he very slowly lowers himself onto his chair, resting on his stumps.

Going back is almost the same except going up the stairs he doesn't have the strength to work along the railing uphill, so he turns around so he's facing away from the stairs, puts his hands behind himself on the first stair and pushes down, lifting his body up to the level of the stair. He repeats this all the way to the top of the stairs, then walks on his hands down the hall to his room. The doorknob on his door is only two feet off the ground. Max always keeps his door locked. Not even Jerry knows what all he's got in there. We know he has a TV and a record player and a bed.

Nobody knows how he lost his legs either. His stumps are perfectly even and flat, so you know there was some kind of amputation performed, but Max is the only one in Max's that won't talk about how he got the way he is. Everyone accepts that. Nobody has ever asked him since I've been around. Maybe he would tell us, but I don't think anybody will ever ask him. It's like when I was a kid and we'd start clubs. The guy who started the club never had to be initiated. He was automatically in the club by virtue of having invented it.

16

Then the basketball season ended. We'd been running Max's about a month when the Warriors lost their final playoff game to the Phoenix Suns in June. It's amazing to me all the things that happened in one basketball season's worth of time. Ann and Jerry split up, Jerry beat Alvin Martin, I end up owning Max's. Some people complain that not enough happens in their life, but I can't complain about that. It seems like every time I put out just a little effort, things start happening so fast I can't stop them even when I want to.

When the Warriors lost, Jerry got depressed. They were still very much his friends, even if they didn't know him. Alvin Martin was named rookie of the year and it seemed to me that Jerry should have felt great about that, since he'd beaten him, but he didn't. He got sick for a couple weeks with the flu and he was in a terrible mood. I guess part of it was being sidetracked from getting his operation. It was the first time Jerry had ever been really depressed in all the time I'd known him. He looked to the future and tried to enjoy the present. So seeing him depressed really got to me. I kept trying to think of ways to help him out but he was oblivious to me.

One night I went up to his room and he was lying on his bed just staring up at the ceiling. He looked really angry.

So I ask him what's wrong. At first he doesn't say anything and then he says he's just tired. He says he just needs a little time to rest. I ask him if he's having pain. He says a little more than usual. I ask him if he wants to see a doctor.

"Yeah," he says, "I want my operation." He says it defiantly, his voice full of passion.

"Well," I say, "it won't be long."

"It'll be forever," he says.

"Aw, Jerry," I tell him, "just another six months. That's not so long."

He starts to cry. He turns over and buries his face in his pillow. His whole body is shaking as he sobs. I want to sit by him and put my hand on his back. I want to comfort him but I'm afraid.

"Hey, Jerry," I say, trying to soothe him.

"I threw so much away!" he screams. Then he turns back over and sits up and wipes his eyes. "I threw away twenty thousand dollars on Ann!" he shouts, shaking his head back and forth. "Twenty thousand dollars, Roary, and she's off in some stinkhole in Oakland! What good did any of it do? I'm no better off than I was when I first met her, and she's worse! What the fuck am I doing?!"

"Look, Jerry," I said, "you did your best. You're always telling me we have to forget the past, well . . ."

"Bullshit," he says, interrupting me. "I don't know shit, Roary. Do you hear me?" Then he says almost to himself, "Everything I touch turns to shit."

"I didn't turn to shit," I say, trying to sound casual but not feeling casual.

That gets him. He starts laughing and I can tell we're gonna have some one-liners.

"That's because," says Jerry, laughing harder, "that's because you were already shit, Roary. I didn't have to do a thing."

17

It took us awhile to get the new Max's running smoothly, but by the end of July we were in high gear and actually making a pretty good profit, which none of us had expected. Edith was a gift from heaven, we gave Bert a raise he should have had six months before, and Jerry seemed to be coming out of his depression slowly but surely. I was still trying to figure out some way to raise money for Jerry's operation but the pressure wasn't as great as before, for some reason. It was the off season and he was making such good money I figured he'd have enough soon anyway.

And then Ann came back. No warning, no phone call, nothing. She just walked into Max's one afternoon and says to Jerry, "Well I'm back." And what did Jerry do? Does he stick to his guns about her kicking, about her not whoring any more before he'd take her back? No. He welcomed her home with open arms. He'd been missing her all along, secretly hoping she'd come back, at least that's the way it seemed because he was so goddamn happy again. He moved out of Max's and they got a new apartment, pretty close to mine on Sixth Avenue.

I couldn't believe it, didn't want to believe it. I wanted Jerry to stick to this dream I had for him, but of course he couldn't. He had to stick to his own dream. But still I couldn't believe he could just take her back without a moment's hesitation, after all she'd done to him, when he *knew* she would keep him from getting his operation. If she had died over in Oakland, Jerry would never have known, and right then I wished she had died.

I had a hard time even being around Jerry for a while after that. He seemed *so* happy. I couldn't figure it out. I avoided him and he didn't seem to mind. He was too busy with Ann again. He really seemed to enjoy himself more, as if he'd been feeling guilty the whole time she'd been gone. Everybody knew it wouldn't be long before she was screwing guys again and shooting up, but nobody said anything about it. I felt like the whole world had just jumped back half a year.

Then about a week after Ann came back, Jerry told me he was going to quit his job at the box factory and just work full time at Max's. It was lunchtime when he told me. I was sitting at the bar eating one of Edith's grinders and Jerry is running around serving beer and as he goes by one time he says, "Hey, Roary, I think I'm gonna quit my job down there."

"What?" I say, trying to keep calm. I want to shout, What about your operation? Have you given up on that too? But I couldn't because I had promised never to tell anybody and Max's was jammed.

"Yeah," he says, stopping in front of me for a minute, smiling that big smile. "I'm tired of running around, Roary. I'm just gonna take it easy, forget about all that other shit."

"Aw, Jerry," I said, feeling suddenly sick, "are you sure?"

"Yeah," he said, shaking his head. "It was all a stupid dream anyway."

That killed me. "Jerry," I said, "we gotta talk."

"Okay, later," he says.

63

I went on a walk and tried to figure out what was happening. I walked down to Golden Gate Park and watched the tennis players. The morning fog had finally burned off and it was starting to get hot. There's almost nothing in bloom in July. There's just a hundred shades of green in the park, and of course tourists and joggers and couples lying around on the grass making out.

The only thing that made any sense to me was that Jerry was giving up, not taking it easy. That's all there was to it. In a way I didn't blame him. After all, what he was trying to do seemed impossible, but I just couldn't accept his giving up. Now I look back and I realize I couldn't accept it because I was counting on Jerry. Jerry was a kind of proof that we all had a chance.

Later on I went back to Max's and when Jerry took a break, he and I went up to his old room and sat on the mattress and I told him I couldn't believe he was giving up when he knew the operation might make him better and take away the pain. "Look," I said, "I'll borrow the money."

"From who?" he said, shaking his head.

"My credit's good at the bank," I said. "I've almost paid off the first loan. I'll say it's for fixing up Max's."

"They won't lend you fifteen thousand dollars," said Jerry "This place is already double-mortgaged."

"But if they would?" I said anxiously, feeling him slipping away.

"I don't know," he said. "Maybe."

"Maybe you shouldn't quit your job at the box factory just yet," I said. "Maybe if you just took a vacation, in case you change your mind."

"Look, Roary," he said, putting a hand on my knee. "I really appreciate your concern for me, but Ann and I decided that one of the problems has always been that I'm not around enough for her. That I've always been working too hard. She needs my time more than my money."

64

"But, Jerry," I said, "that doesn't mean you still can't get the operation."

"We'll see," he says, standing up and stretching. "Anything can happen, Roary."

"If you really want it to," I said bitterly.

"Right," he said, walking out. "Catch you later."

I knew he hadn't heard the bitterness in my voice. He was closing off to me. He was throwing it all away and I knew it couldn't just be Ann. I knew he had to be afraid of something, but I couldn't figure out what he was afraid of.

18

So Jerry quit his job and he and Ann would go to movies and out to dinner fairly often. They even went away for a weekend one time. But I could tell things weren't working out.

Ann almost never came into Max's except when she needed money. She was supposedly looking for a job, but she was so busy spending Jerry's money I doubt she had much time to look for work.

She'd come in to Max's quietly, almost ashamed, walk to the end of the bar and sit waiting for Jerry if he wasn't already there. When Jerry came back from serving a table, *he'd* kiss her and then they'd whisper back and forth, which may have seemed romantic if you didn't know the inside story, and then Jerry would slip her twenty dollars or fifty dollars, *then* she'd kiss him and walk out of the place with a big smile on her face. We all knew she wasn't buying books or food or new clothes with that money. Everybody in Max's, except maybe Stinky, the eternal optimist, knew that she was spending the money on junk. But Jerry didn't seem to care about that any more.

Ann wasn't a bad person, you could see that, and she didn't really hurt anybody that didn't want to be hurt. I saw that finally because I realized Jerry was asking for everything she did to him. And she hurt me because I cared about Jerry. It was like caring for someone who likes to run in front of moving cars.

Then one afternoon, Ann's Oakland pimp shows up at Max's. He's one of the biggest men I've ever seen. I'd guess he was six feet six inches tall, probably close to 250 pounds of solid muscle, well-defined weightlifting muscle. And handsome too, like a movie star. Not real dark and with kind of Latin features, like maybe his mother was Mexican and his father was black. He's got a beautiful smile and his eyes are half closed, but he doesn't wear shades, which is almost unheard of among pimps. He's wearing a fancy purple net tee-shirt that shows off his incredible chest and shoulders, and I can't help wondering why he's not playing professional football and killing guys legally. Bad knees probably.

Benny and the other pimp that hangs out at Max's, Marvin Clark, are just dazzled beyond words to have such a big-time pimp visiting. Benny and Marvin could be twins. The skinny black twins in identical three-piece suits, gray usually, big round sunglasses and elevator shoes about four inches high. Compared to Ann's pimp they're both really dark.

When he came through the door, Max's went quiet. There was a pretty good crowd too, the after-lunch bunch, and it's a noisy crowd, but when this guy came in we could all suddenly hear our hearts beating.

Benny and Marvin floated up to him like he was some kind of visiting god. They jived around, sort of bowed and scraped a little, he allowed them to slap his hand gently and they talked for a moment so low I couldn't believe they could really be hearing each other. Then he moves away from them, moving soundlessly, and I see he's wearing fancy running shoes, not elevators. He comes over to the bar, just about dead center where Jerry is and he smiles at Jerry and says,

66

"How do you do, Mr. Maxwell. I'm Lucius Porter, a friend of Ann's."

Jerry knew who the guy was but he didn't bat an eyelash while the guy introduced himself. "I believe," says Lucius, his voice deep and so resonant you expect him to start singing, "that Ann has a ring of mine, which I place a rather high value on. If you'd be so kind as to tell me where I might find her, I'd deeply appreciate it." Everybody in Max's is listening to him talk.

I'm sitting ten feet away and I can hear the murder in his voice. As he speaks his arm muscles flex and unflex and I got the feeling he was winding himself up, getting ready to tear Jerry into little pieces.

Jerry smiles at him, not a nervous smile, a very calm, in-control smile. Jerry has more guts at the weirdest times than anybody I know. He can't go to a goddamn doctor by himself, but here's a monster breathing in his face and Jerry just smiles. It's that smile I've only seen a few times but it always means he's ready for action. "I didn't think that ring was real," said Jerry, quietly, still smiling.

"It is a ring of infinite worth," said Lucius, flexing faster, his hands forming fists. "I would like it back."

"Well, I'll get it for you," said Jerry, casually going into his glass-drying routine. "I think she already hocked it, but if she didn't, I'll get it for you."

"If you don't," says Lucius, his smile fading, "I'll kill you." Then his smile comes back full force.

"Oh," said Jerry, shaking his head sadly, putting down the glass he's working on, "I wish you hadn't said that. That kind of thing isn't allowed in Max's. You'll have to leave. I'm sorry, but . . . you understand."

Lucius laughs. He puts his head back and really laughs, the flexing stops. "You are quite the fool," he says. "A goodly fool, though. I would I were not on such an irrevocable course. We might have been friends."

I swear to God he said that. He talked like he was in a Shakespearean play or something.

Jerry laughs too, but the laugh isn't real. He cuts it short and says, "Get outta here."

Lucius bows, then starts to leave, but he stops by the door and says to Jerry, "Tomorrow you will bring the ring. I'll be here at noon." Then he walks out and everybody in Max's starts talking at the same time.

Benny comes bopping over to the bar and beams at Jerry. "Oh, preacher," he says, "you're in shit shape now. Old Lucius is just itching to smash you, boy. He don't like anybody taking his women, but when you go messin with his rocks you might as well be jumpin off the bridge."

Jerry just ignores Benny, throws down his towel and runs out after Lucius. "Hey, Jerry," I say as he goes by, but he ignores me. I get up and go after him. I'm scared to death what might happen. Just as I come out the door, Jerry has caught up to Lucius about fifty yards down the street. I'm holding my breath. Jerry's this little tiny white person standing by this huge dark person and it looks like Lucius could squish him with a couple fingers. Jerry reaches toward Lucius and Lucius takes something from Jerry's hand and then walks away. I guess Jerry had the ring all the time. I guess he didn't want the guys in Max's to see him giving in to Lucius.

When Jerry comes back inside, Wendel Porter, a guy with muscular dystrophy who *never* talks says, "What happened, Jerry?"

"Nothing," said Jerry, going back to work.

"He gonna come back and kill you?" asks Wendel.

"No," said Jerry, coming back to Wendel and putting a hand on the old guy's shoulder. "Don't worry about it, champ, he's not coming back."

But, boy, Max's was never so full as it was the next day at noon. Standing room only. And of course Lucius didn't show up and everybody thought Jerry had scared him off somehow.

19

Then about three days later, I open up at eleven as usual, Edith comes in at eleven-thirty and goes into her super sandwich routine and Max's is jammed. It's one of those freak scorching afternoons where we might as well be in Missouri. Max's is cool and dark and the beer is cold, so everybody flocks in. Plus, Edith's sandwiches were starting to get a reputation and we were getting new people in for lunch all the time.

Jerry was supposed to be there a little before noon but he didn't show up. I'm going nuts shuffling around trying to serve beer and hand out sandwiches, sweating like crazy. My neck is killing me and by twelve-thirty I'm tempted to close Max's for the day. Luckily Max was able to get hold of Bert and he came in just as I was about to collapse.

"Where's Jerry?" he says, throwing off his sweatshirt and going to work.

"Christ if I know," I say, sitting down behind the bar as fast as I can. "He didn't call or anything."

Being a bartender in Max's is not an easy job. You not only have to work behind the bar but you have to roam out among the tables since most of the guys can't get back and forth to the bar very easily, especially with a pitcher of beer and a sandwich or two. Most of the time it's no problem for one guy, but with lunchtime business getting so good we were seriously considering getting more help.

"That's just not like Jerry," says Bert, coming over to have a beer with me after the lunch rush was over.

"Oh, he's been weird lately," I said, though that was mainly from my point of view and nobody else's.

"Still, he would have called, don't you think?" said Bert, winking at Edith as she goes by. I like Bert. He's got a really nice relaxed way about him. I don't know anybody as kind, really, as Bert. He's also really strong, which somehow makes his being kind easy. He's your classic gentle giant. He lifts weights and swims all the time. He swims across the bay every year with the Aquatic Club. He was married for seven years and had a couple kids, but when he got divorced the kids stayed with his wife in Los Angeles. He takes a month off every summer and goes camping with his kids.

"Yeah," I say, "Max tried calling him but nobody answered."

"That worries me just a little," said Bert. "Maybe you oughta go over there."

"I don't know," I said. I was really pissed off at Jerry for not coming in, not even calling so we could get somebody else. I was so mad and my neck was so sore I didn't even consider that he might have had a good reason for not coming in.

"Well, then, you watch the bar and I'll run over there," says Bert, grabbing his sweatshirt.

"No, I'll go," I say. I wasn't in any shape to tend bar anyway. Every time I picked up a pitcher of beer my neck hurt. I stalled around for another ten minutes, tried calling Jerry again, and then I started over there. I'd only seen their new apartment once right after they moved in, but I didn't go there at all after that. I never even walked by it.

On the way over I thought of what I was going to say. I rehearsed it. "You may be part owner of Max's, Jerry, and you may be feeling low, but that doesn't mean you don't have a responsibility to call if . . ." Somehow that seemed like a ridiculous thing to say to the most responsible person I've ever known. Jerry just wouldn't not call.

People had set up sprinklers on the sidewalk for their kids to play in, so I got pretty soaked on the way over. It was either that or go out in the street, which I'm not about to do with my speed, besides it was so hot I was glad to get wet.

Every time I went through a sprinkler the kids would shriek and laugh, which made me feel pretty good because I love kids, though they're usually just afraid of me.

Anyway, by the time I got to Jerry's apartment building I wasn't angry any more. I was a little worried, like Bert. I go up the stairs slowly, even slower than usual. Jerry's place is on the third floor. It's a four-story apartment building, very old like mine and musty-smelling.

When I got to the third floor I was actually a little scared. I walk down the hall to Jerry's apartment and I'm straining to hear if anybody's home. I don't hear anything, but the door is open a little. That's nothing, Jerry always leaves his door open a little when he's home. I knock. Nobody answers. Every sound I make seems so loud because the old place echoes everything I do. I can't even hear traffic it's so quiet.

"Jerry?" I say. Nothing. "Ann?" I say. I wait a minute, then I say louder, "Jerry?"

Then I hear something, a scraping noise. It sends a chill up my spine. "Jerry?" I say.

Then I hear the scraping again. It sounds like a chair being pushed along the floor. Then a glass something falls and breaks. "Jerry!" I call. I'm afraid to open the door. I hear the scraping again.

"Jerry!" I scream and I push the door open.

Jesus Christ, I'll never forget that scene. Jerry is on the floor pushing a chair towards the door. The apartment looks like a bomb hit it. Jerry's bleeding at the mouth and his face is all cut and bruised. He's dragging himself towards the door, his mouth working but no sound is coming out. It looks like his legs are broken.

I get to him and get down on my knees and lift him up. He's so torn up I start to cry. He says, "Water," whispering it. I lift him up and lay him on the couch and go get him a glass of water. When I come back with the water I see his neck. There's two huge rope burns around it.

I go to the phone to call an ambulance and Jerry throws

the glass of water at me and it breaks on the floor at my feet. I look at him and he's waving me back to him. I go over to him. "Jerry, you need a doctor," I tell him. "I'm calling an ambulance." I'm so scared he might be dying, my whole body is shaking.

"No doctor," he whispers, his eyes all bloodshot and wild. "No police. Nobody."

"Aw Christ, Jerry, you're hurt bad."

He shakes his head. "Water," he whispers again.

Well, I finally got Bert over there and we finally convinced Jerry to let us take him to a doctor that evening. I thought Jerry's legs were broken but miraculously they were just so badly bruised he couldn't walk. His vocal cords were severely bruised too, not broken, and though he had been knocked unconscious he didn't have a fracture when we got him x-rayed the next day.

What happened was Lucius came in with two friends and they beat Jerry up. Jerry says he could have handled Lucius but not all three of them. He said he broke one guy's jaw and knocked the other guy cold before they knocked him out. I believe him. He doesn't know why they didn't kill him. Maybe Ann asked them not to. She went with them. In fact, she was all packed and waiting to go. She told Jerry she was going back to Lucius because it made life easier. He gave her the junk. She didn't have to hustle for it.

20

So Bert and I moved Jerry back to his room upstairs in Max's and I took care of him until he could walk again. Every day I'd run a hot bath and then help him out of bed, he'd put his

72

arm around my shoulder and I'd drag him down the hall and help him into the tub. Then I'd sit on the toilet and read *Sports Illustrated* to him. Then after his bath I'd give him a leg massage like the doctor showed me.

He could make it down the hall by himself after about ten days. His voice took almost a month to come back, and it was really low at first. He couldn't remember them putting the rope around his neck or them kicking his legs, so it must have been when he was out cold.

Only Bert and I knew what happened. Jerry begged us not to tell anyone. The doctor we got sees guys beat up all the time, so he didn't know Jerry from some drunk who got rolled a little harder than usual. And whenever one of the guys in Max's asked what happened to Jerry, we just said he had a bad fall.

But when Jerry started to walk and talk again, he didn't get mad. He seemed so passive now, almost docile. It was like they'd kicked the spirit out of him. I couldn't stand seeing him so demoralized. I tried to get him angry or happy or anything, but he wasn't interested.

One afternoon I was in his room and I asked him if he wanted to go get Lucius. I don't know why I thought of it but I did. Maybe because I wanted Jerry to want to get him.

"No," said Jerry, quietly. "I've got nothing against him."

"What are you talking about!" I said. "Are you crazy? The bastard almost killed you!"

"I think Ann loves him," said Jerry, looking down at his lap.

"Oh Christ, Jerry, she's a junky. She doesn't know what she loves. If she loved him, why did she keep coming back to you?"

"I don't know," said Jerry, sighing. He sighed all the time now and it drove me crazy.

"Well what do you think?" I said, getting really pissed off.

"I don't know," he says, lying down and closing his eyes.

"Aw come on, Jerry! Quit being such a basket case!

Where's your balls?" I was trying to get him out of that mon-otone self-pity.

"No balls," he says weakly. "No balls, Roary."

"You're a dumb shit," I said.

"I know," he said.

"Aw cut it out, Jerry!" I say.

"I'm sorry," he says.

It went on like that for a month after they beat him. He could walk and talk but he wasn't Jerry. I tried every day, all kinds of ways to snap him out of it, but nothing seemed to work.

Jerry played cards with me, with Bert, with the guys, even with Max a couple times, but that was about all he did, that and sleep. He stopped shaving, got pretty scruffy-looking. Looked more like one of the guys. I figured he'd start playing basketball again once his legs were better and that would wake him up if nothing else did, but when the doctor told him to go ahead and exercise, Jerry didn't. I couldn't believe it. "Jerry," I said, "basketball. Nothing to do all day if you want but play basketball."

"Maybe later," he said, shuffling the cards.

"Come on, Jerry," I said. "*I'll* play with you." That would have been a very funny joke a month before.

"No," he said, "maybe later."

But he wouldn't play. Jerry wouldn't play ball. I knew he was dying then.

21

In the middle of August, Jackson Fellows started working at Max's to fill in while Bert went off to see his kids for a month. Jackson is a friend of Bert's from the Aquatic Club and among other things he's the funniest person I've ever known. He can make anybody laugh. I've seen him walk into Max's on the gloomiest day when nobody is smiling and within five minutes he'll have guys falling out of their chairs, Edith laughing so hard she's crying and Blue Louis with his mouth wide open, his whole body shaking but no sound coming out because he's lost his breath from laughter, and it really is a miracle we haven't had several heart attacks since Jackson came on the scene.

Jackson is tall and muscular, not as broad-shouldered as Bert but just as imposing. He's got a huge Afro, at least six inches thick, and I think he's really handsome, but he's so famous around Max's for being funny, most people don't think of him as being handsome. He has big brown eyes and well-defined dimples, so when he smiles you have to smile at his smile if nothing else.

He really saved Max's, brought so much humor and joy to the place it was like Christmas had come. Christ, he and Edith would get going teasing each other and I'd laugh until my head was gonna fall off. Even old Jerry had to laugh. You could see him trying not to, but Jackson would get him anyway. He'd concentrate on Jerry until finally, finally Jerry would laugh too.

But Jackson couldn't snap Jerry out of his depression. Jerry would work his shift and Max's would get very quiet, very subdued. People whispered, like it was a library. A bartender can do that, control the mood, especially at a place like Max's where the customers are depending on the guy for more than just drinks.

After about a week on the job, Jackson ran Benny out of Max's. A few guys resented that because Benny was their pimp, but Jackson didn't have much of a sense of humor when it came to pimps. He wasn't a religious nut or anything, he just couldn't stand guys like Benny.

I was too preoccupied with Jerry to really enjoy Jackson as much as I should have, but Jerry was so pale and lethargic I couldn't stop worrying about him. I got him to go to the Med

Center, and the doctor there said Jerry had low blood sugar and wasn't getting sufficient protein.

So Edith would fix him soup and the best sandwiches in the world and he'd hardly touch them. It was driving me crazy. What he needed was a psychiatrist or something but he didn't have the will to think of it. He lost so much weight his cheeks started to cave in. I really thought he was going to just keel over and die.

I finally got up the nerve one night when we were playing cards in his room. I said, trying to be casual about it, "Maybe you oughta see a psychologist or something."

"No," he said, "I'm just tired, Roary."

"Aw Jerry, you're doing this to yourself," I said. "You're starving yourself."

He looks at me for a minute with a sort of glazed expression and then he says, "No, Roary, I'm just not hungry."

"Why do you think that is?" I ask.

"I don't know," he says. "I have no idea."

The next afternoon I'm talking to Jackson about Jerry and for some reason I let slip that Jerry beat Alvin Martin. Jackson looks at me funny. "You feeling okay, Roary? I think maybe you're wearing too many clothes on hot days. That'll drive you crazy in a minute."

"It's true," I said. Then I told him the whole story, everything except about the operation. I wanted to tell him about that too, but I couldn't.

"That's hard to believe," says Jackson. "Man, Jerry doesn't look like he could walk around the block right now."

"He probably couldn't," I said.

"Well, he'll break out of it," said Jackson, dropping a glass and catching it before it hit the bar. "Hell, I was once so depressed nothing could cheer me up. And understanding *why* I was depressed didn't help either. In fact, understanding why was part of the problem."

"How come?" I said.

"You trying to get me depressed again?" says Jackson, glaring at me. "Man, I was so depressed I set the world's record for lying on the floor on my back, fully clothed, one shoe off, one shoe on. I lay there for three days trying to figure out why I was bothering to put on my shoes."

"So how'd you finally break out of it?" I asked, trying to stay serious.

"Oh, then I fell in love and that was all I needed," he said, grinning. "Do it every time, Roary."

"Yeah," I said, "but how's Jerry gonna fall in love moping around Max's?"

"Oh, I don't know," says Jackson, batting his eyelashes at me and raising his voice. "Jes look at the bartender."

"Seriously," I said.

"Listen, Roary," he said, leaning over towards me and giving me such an overly serious look I can't help but laugh a little. "If somewhere inside he's still burning, he'll make it. Don't worry about it. And don't ask me to be serious more than once a day. It gives me a stomachache."

I spent all day thinking of ways to get the money for his operation, but there was just no way I could think of. Then one afternoon I was up in Jerry's room and I picked up his newest *Sports Illustrated*, which he hadn't even opened yet, and there was Alvin Martin on the front cover, five feet off the ground, dunking the ball. The caption underneath the picture said: "Is This Man Worth Three Million Dollars?" And then I knew where I was going to get the money.

22

First I had to find out where Alvin lived. It's not so easy finding out where a celebrity lives, I discovered. I called the Warriors office and told them I wanted to contact Alvin Martin and they told me to send a letter to them and they would forward it, but I wasn't about to write him a letter. The article in *Sports Illustrated* said he lived in Palo Alto, so I got a Palo Alto phone book and looked him up, but all three Alvin Martin's I called weren't the right one. I don't know what I would have said if I had gotten *the* Alvin Martin, but to these guys I said, "Hi, I'm a reporter for the *Chronicle*. Is this the home of Alvin Martin who plays for the Warriors?" Pretty bad I admit. Two people just said no, and one guy said, "Don't I wish."

There was a picture in *Sports Illustrated* of Alvin jogging up the driveway leading to his house and the article said he lived in an exclusive neighborhood, so I figured if I could get somebody to drive me around and we really worked at it, we could spot the place.

The only guy I know who drives is Jackson. I didn't think he'd want to do it since he'd only known me for a few weeks, but when I asked him he said sure. So on a hot smoggy Saturday we drove down to Palo Alto in Jackson's sky-blue '57 Dodge and cruised all over, stopping at gas stations and asking where we could find the exclusive neighborhoods. One guy was sort of suspicious and asked us why we wanted to know. Jackson looks at the guy for a second and then, sounding completely serious, he says, "To rape, steal and pillage, man. What did you think we were gonna do? Sightsee?"

Then when we'd get into a nice neighborhood, we'd stop whenever we saw kids playing and Jackson would ask them if they knew where Alvin Martin lived. We did that all day with no luck.

Jackson was really nice about the whole thing, never even asked me why I was doing it or anything. "Now, Roary," he says "when we find him he's gonna be buggin me for my autograph, you know, so I'm countin on you to explain the situation to him."

"What's the situation?" I asked, walking into it as usual.

"About the thing," says Jackson, wrinkling his brow.

"What thing?"

"You know . . . about God."

"What are you talking about?" I ask him, getting totally confused.

"It's off between us," says Jackson, his lips quivering. "I thought I could do it, you know . . . go bispiritual, but like I chickened out at the last minute because, What if the experience, you know, turned me off to women? I mean I'd just die."

"Yeah, but what does that have to do with not giving Alvin Martin your autograph?" I ask.

"You still back on that?" says Jackson, slapping my knee. "Man, that joke was sunk before it ever floated. You gotta be movin man, keep the ideas jumpin, the words flowin, you gotta move ahead fast or those bad crummy terrible jokes sneak up and crush you from behind."

Sometimes I'm not sure what Jackson is talking about, but if I have to be cooped up in a car all day I can't think of anybody better to do it with than Jackson.

I asked him not to tell Jerry about what we'd been doing and he looks puzzled for a minute and says, "Jerry who?"

We spent all day Sunday looking too, but we still didn't find it. When we got back to Max's on Sunday evening I tried to pay Jackson for his trouble, but he pretended to be insulted and shocked and then he put his head down on the steering wheel and actually got himself to cry. Like I say, the guy should be onstage. Then suddenly he sits up and says real fast, "Gimme five for gas."

I slept like a log Sunday night. I was emotionally and physically exhausted, not to mention extremely depressed. I woke up late Monday morning and was just wandering around my apartment, not really wanting to go into Max's and see Jerry moping around, when somebody knocks on the door. It's Jackson.

He's wearing a very fancy green suit and looks very flashy. "Hey, Roary," he says, holding out his palms to me.

79

"Hey, Jackson," I say, slapping his palms lightly. I'm not in a very good mood and he obviously is.

"You ready to go?" he says, slapping mine hard.

"Go where?" I ask, trying to remember what I'd forgotten about.

"To Alvin Martin's," says Jackson, giving me a look like I'm an idiot for not knowing.

"You gotta work today, don't you?" I ask.

"Tonight," he says, casually. "How much time you need? Come on, boy, get your clothes on."

"But we don't even know where he lives," I say, flopping down on my couch.

"We *didn't* know where he lives," says Jackson. "We *do* now."

"We do?" I say, getting up as fast as I can.

"In fact, he's expecting us at one o'clock, so get your booties on, slick down your mop and let's boogie."

"But how? How?" I ask, trying not to shout.

Jackson swells himself up to his full height, then goes up onto his toes so he's a good six foot six. "Hello," he says in a soft sincere voice. "Ma'am, my name is Jackson Fellows, played basketball with Alvin Martin at UCLA. Been trying to get in touch with the man but he's either the most unlisted dude in the world or I can't spell Martin. Thought I'd check with y'all here at the team office. I'm playin for New Orleans this season. You got his number handy?"

"And then what?" I ask, my heart pounding.

"And then," says Jackson, coming down off his toes, "I called him up and made us an appointment, so unless you wanna go looking like an ad for Fruit of the Loom, why don't you get your ass *dressed!*"

23

On the way down I tried to find out what Jackson had said to Alvin Martin on the phone, but he kept jiving with me and turning everything I said into a comedy routine, so I quit asking and tried to figure out what I was going to say to Alvin Martin.

We never could have found the place by just driving around. For one thing, Alvin lives in Atherton, which is five or ten miles from Palo Alto, and besides, the house is up a long private drive that doesn't look anything like the *Sports Illustrated* picture.

I'm wearing my very best clothes, an old gray suit that's too small for me, and my hair is greased down, but I know I still look terrible. There's nothing I can do about it.

The funny thing was, I wasn't scared at all the whole way down. But the minute we start up the driveway I suddenly realize what I'm doing and I realize I'm out of my mind! I can't just drive up to Alvin Martin's, walk in and ask him for money. I can't believe I'm doing this. I start to feel sick and trembly like I have a fever. "Jackson," I say, looking out the window at this incredible estate. "Jackson, stop the car."

"What's wrong?" says Jackson, putting on the brakes. "You sick, Roary?"

"Jackson, I can't do this. Let's just get out of here, okay?" I say, breathing hard.

"Can't do what?" says Jackson, and I can hear he's dead serious.

"I can't go see Alvin like this."

"Now, wait a minute," says Jackson, jerking on the hand brake. I can tell he's pissed off. I've never seen him so mad.

He sits there for a minute getting control of himself and then he turns to me and says, "Look, Roary, it isn't any of my business *what* you want to say to Alvin Martin, but I'll be damned if I'm gonna turn around after all the bullshit I've been through to get you here."

"I'm sorry," I said.

"Don't be sorry," says Jackson, "just don't quit on me like this." He lets off the brake and we start forward again slowly.

"What did you say on the phone to him?" I ask.

"I told him some jokes, dropped a few names of people I know I thought he might know, then I told him I had a friend who desperately needed to speak to him and he said come on down. So here we are."

And there we were, parked in front of a beautiful house surrounded by this perfect Japanese garden. There was a little stream running by the house and two old Japanese gardeners raking the path and pulling weeds.

"You ready?" asked Jackson.

"Not really," I said.

"Good," he says, smiling at me. "It's never good to be overprepared. You want to leave a little room to improvise."

We get out of the car and start up the gravel path to the front door. Everything was Japanese. The house was modern but definitely Japanese style, built completely of redwood, and the Japanese garden wasn't just in front but went all around the place. It didn't really fit with what I'd expected. I'd sort of imagined a big three-story mansion, almost like a castle, and a big driveway full of Cadillacs and Rolls-Royces. But it was just the opposite, very quiet, big but simple.

Jackson rang the bell and after about ten seconds I hear footsteps. It's an oversized door, at least eight feet tall, and when the door opened I had my eyes focused at about six or seven feet expecting Alvin to be there, but instead, dropping down about two feet here's this very beautiful Japanese woman, with long black hair. She smiles at me, doesn't blink an eye at how ugly I must seem to her. "Come in, come in," she says. "I'll tell Al you're here."

We follow her inside and she leaves us standing in a wide entranceway. There's a Japanese painting of a man fishing from a little boat on one wall, and straight ahead of us in the middle of a large open area there's a tall wooden sculpture of a naked native sort of guy dancing. He's balanced on one leg and his other leg is twisting out behind him and his arms are reaching up towards the ceiling. Jackson sees me looking at it and whispers, "One of my earlier works. I'm into plastics now." I'm too nervous to ask him what he's talking about, I figure he's joking, so I just say uh huh and try to stop breathing so hard.

Then a minute or so later, Alvin Martin comes walking down the hall towards us. He's wearing this beautiful African robe, black, purple and white, and he looks like a goddamn prince. He comes up to us and he and Jackson shake hands about five different ways and say hi man how you doin, and then Alvin turns to me and we shake hands the regular way. Apparently he doesn't remember me.

"Pleased to meet you," says Alvin, giving me a curious sort of smile.

"My name is Roary," I say. Then I just blurt it out. "I was with Jerry, the guy with the limp, the day you guys had that one-on-one at the Pavilion?"

"Oh yeah," said Alvin, breaking into a big smile. "I thought you looked familiar." Then he sighed and his smile faded a little. "Hey man, I'm really sorry about the things I said that day. I really didn't mean it, you know."

"Oh that's okay," I say. It's not okay but at least he remembers me.

"How is Jerry?" he asks, like they were old friends or something.

"Not so good," I said.

"That's too bad," said Alvin, turning to Jackson. "Hey, how about we have a little drink?"

"You read my mind," said Jackson.

"Okay," I mumble.

We follow Alvin through the living room and out into a

garden that the house surrounds. There's a pond full of big colorful carp, a little waterfall, some miniature pine trees. He leaves us sitting on a stone bench by the pond and goes back inside to get our drinks.

I'm totally dazed. I can't really think what to say next. Jackson nudges me. "You want to talk to him alone, don't you?"

"I don't know," I say. "I don't know what to do exactly."

"I'll see what I can do," he says, getting up and going into the house before I can stop him.

The thing was, I knew inside what I wanted to say, but putting it into words seemed impossible. I wanted to say, "Jerry needs money for an operation. Can you lend it to me? I'll pay you back." But that sounds pretty weak if you don't know the whole story first.

Alvin came back out alone, handed me a beer and then sat down beside me. I sipped the beer and he watched me for a second, then he shook his head and broke into a laugh. "You know," he said, "I almost went down to Edison Park to look for your buddy. I couldn't get over that game we played. I still think about it sometimes. It was unbelievable. I don't think he could do that again in a million years."

"Well, you're probably right," I say, "since he doesn't play any more."

"Oh, I don't believe that," said Alvin. "A dude plays like that cause he's addicted to the game. Can't help but play."

"Well, he doesn't play any more," I said. "Hasn't played in months."

Alvin looks at me and says, "Tell me the story."

I told him everything from the very start on up until right then. I told him about Ann and Max and Lucius and even about Valerie. I hadn't told anyone any of this stuff for so long it just poured out of me. I must have talked for an hour. And then I told him about Jerry visiting Dr. Carlton and how Jerry didn't have the money for the operation.

Alvin sat quietly the whole time, never interrupting. A few

times he'd shake his head slowly or sigh, but that was it. I just blabbed and blabbed. When I finished he just sat there for a while and then he said very seriously, "I'll be honest with you, Roary, if I hadn't played with that dude, this all wouldn't mean that much to me. Now, that may sound cruel, but the fact is I know stories that make Jerry's sound like a picnic. There's so much shit out there it's beyond belief. I'm numb to most of it now. I help my friends and I spend my money on a couple projects I hope will help some people, but if I shelled out for every sob story I've heard, I'd a been broke before I ever made a dime." He sighs and looks down at his hands. "But," he says, looking up at me, "that little bastard kicked my ass and I know it doesn't make a whole lot of sense, but I can't get it out of my head that he somehow deserves another shot. And if he can get it with two good legs, if it's in my power to give him that shot, then I'll do it."

"You will?" I said, practically falling off the bench.

"But I want you to know something, Roary, and I want Jerry to know it too," he says, glaring at me. "I'm not doing this out of pity. This is a loan which I'm giving you because I want him walking right the next time we play. You dig?"

"Okay," I said, "I'll tell him."

Then Alvin breaks into a smile and says, "That dude is either a great little ball player, or the luckiest fool in the world."

24

Riding back to San Francisco with Jackson was probably the happiest I'd been since I was a little kid. We joked around all the way home and of course I had to tell him about the operation then, but he'd already pretty much figured it out, so I wasn't really breaking my promise to Jerry any more than I already had. Besides, I thought, what difference did it make now that Alvin was going to lend us the money?

Jackson dropped me at my apartment and then he zipped over to Max's to relieve Jerry. We had supposedly gone fishing for the weekend. I changed my clothes and got over to Max's fifteen minutes later. I was bursting, that's the only way I can describe it. I took a deep breath, told myself to calm down, stepped on the welcome mat and the big door swung open.

"Hello, Roary," says Max. He's sipping a beer and finishing off a cigar. Max smokes a cigar about once a week. As I come up to him I wonder if he has any idea about what's been going on.

"Hey, Max," I say. I wait to see if he has anything else to say to me, since this is the first hello from him I've gotten in three weeks, but he doesn't say anything else, so I wave hello to Jackson and then go upstairs. Jerry's door is open and I can hear him moving around.

"Hey, Jerry," I say, my voice quivering a little. I cough and clear my throat.

"Hey, Roary, how you doing?" he says, flopping down on his bed. "You guys have a nice weekend?"

"Great," I say, trying to figure out how to tell him.

"You wanna play cards?" he asks.

"Sure," I say. I just want to blurt it out, but for some reason that doesn't seem appropriate.

I sit down on his bed and he deals out a hand of gin rummy. I look at him and I can't stand it. I throw the cards down.

"What's a matter?" he says. "Lousy hand?"

"Jerry," I say, "I got the money for your operation!"

He sits there for about a minute. Then he says very quietly, "Where?"

"I went to see Alvin Martin. He said he'd lend you the money."

86

Jerry's face starts to get a little red. "You didn't, Roary," he says.

"I did, Jerry," I say. "I saw him today, a couple hours ago."

"Cut the bullshit, Roary," he says, looking at his cards. "I'm not in the right mood, okay? Let's play."

"Jerry!" I shout, "I saw him! Really! He said he'd do whatever was in his power . . ."

"Roary," he says, cutting me off, a strange look on his face, "I don't believe you. If you don't want to play cards I'll play solitaire." He gathers up the cards and starts shuffling them.

I can't believe this. "Aw come on, Jerry," I say, standing up. His room seems so small and stuffy. His whole life seems so stagnant to me. "I swear to God, Jerry, he said he'd lend us the money!"

Jerry just sits there and then he gets a sort of sneer on his face. "You begged him, right? You told him I was a poor helpless cripple. You gave him a sob story, didn't you, Roary?"

"I told him the truth, Jerry!" I say. "What are you anyway, sick in the head? He's not giving you anything! He's lending you the money because he wants to play you again, because he wants to see if you're really any good. That's what he told me to tell you."

"I'm not a cripple, Roary," he says calmly. "I'm not a beggar either."

"So what?" I said, really starting to lose control. "If you turn this down, Jerry, you're worse than a cripple, you're a loser!"

"Fuck you," says Jerry, mumbling. "Just fuck you."

"Aw Jerry, I'm sorry," I say. "I just wanted to help you."

"Thanks for nothing," he says.

"Jerry," I say, "I can't believe this. I can't believe you mean that. You can't give up like this. You can't quit on me now."

"Who said I'm quitting?" he says, giving me this very righteous look. "Maybe I'm just growing up, Roary. Maybe the Jerry we used to know is finally dead. This Jerry doesn't live fantasies any more. He stopped kidding himself. He stopped all that shit and he's adjusting to reality and it's a little hard, Roary, so he's depressed right now, but he'll get happy again and he'll *accept* himself. Why don't you help him out, Roary, and accept him for what he is, a man with a bad leg, who works in a bar and gets through life, this life, Roary, not a dream world, not playgrounds turning into Madison Square Garden, not whore girlfriends turning into virgin pompom girls. Real, Roary. And until you're ready to accept that, go fuck yourself and quit fucking with me."

"Jerry," I say, "wouldn't you like to walk right, with no pain, if you could?"

"It's not important, Roary. Those bastards almost killed me! I was walking around still thinking I was Superman caught in the body of a jerky little gimp. Well, that's bullshit. I'm Jerry caught in the body of Jerry."

I didn't know what to say. I kept thinking, Why didn't I go to Alvin Martin's two months ago. Because I didn't think of it, that's why. But why didn't I think of it? Because I'm an idiot, that's why.

"Go away, Roary," says Jerry. "I'll see you tomorrow."

"Okay," I said. I felt numb. I started to walk out.

"Hey," said Jerry, sounding more like the Jerry I knew. "Did you really go see him?"

"Yeah," I said.

"What was it like, his house?" He looks just like a kid now.

I told him about the place. I couldn't look at him as I talked. I looked at my hands. "It was Japanese," I said. "Very beautiful. He had some African statues and he was wearing an African gown."

"Hmm," said Jerry, nodding at me.

"Fuck you," I said, and I walked away.

25

Well, I felt like leaving town forever that night. I kept telling myself to calm down, take it as a lesson. Don't pin your hopes on somebody else. But I didn't really believe Jerry would turn down the chance for an operation. I decided it must have been the *way* I told him about getting the money that had upset him. I figured he'd change his mind in a day or so if I just didn't make a big deal about it.

So I didn't say another word about it for the next few days. I told Jackson not to say anything either and not to tell anybody about it and he said okay, though he kept giving me weird looks. Jerry seemed to be making an effort to be more energetic, like he was determined to prove he could come back all by himself, operation or not.

So Thursday evening around seven, we're all sitting around the bar listening to Jackson tell the story of his first love affair. When he was six years old he fell in love with a manikin in the window at Saks Fifth Avenue. She was tall and blond and she was wearing a sexy white tennis outfit, showing off a lot of leg. "The way she smiled at me," says Jackson, "the way her breasts seemed about to jump out of her blouse was downright pornographic." Jackson said he'd take the bus downtown every day to stare at her. He had to lie to his mother about where he was going because she would have died if she knew he was seeing a white woman. Then one day he arrived at Saks to find his lover's outfit had been changed to a sequin evening gown and he was totally crushed. "Suddenly my dream girl looked just like a two-dollar whore," says Jackson, wiping an imaginary tear off his cheek.

Jerry asked him how he knew what a whore looked like at

age six, and Jackson said you'd be surprised how many six-year-old whores there are running around.

So we were in the midst of all that when Alvin Martin walks into Max's. I'm speechless and Jerry looks like he's seen a ghost. Jackson's the only one who could talk. "Welcome to Max's, brother," he says, grinning at Alvin. "What can I get you?"

"Nothin right now," says Alvin. He's wearing flashy blue pants, a white shirt and black tie and a matching blue sports jacket. He looks like he just came from some formal affair. "Hello, Roary," he says, shaking my hand.

"Hi," I say, forcing a smile and then catching myself before the smile got out of hand.

"Hello, Jerry," he says, very quietly.

"Hi," says Jerry, red in the face.

"Could I speak to you two alone somewhere?" he says, obviously uncomfortable.

"Sure," I say, glancing at Jerry. He's staring at Alvin, totally hypnotized.

So we all go up to Jerry's room. Jerry was trembling, so was I. I sat down on the bed and Jerry sat beside me. Alvin sat in the chair and stretched his long legs out towards the door. I felt like I was back in third grade about to be bawled out for breaking something.

"So," says Alvin, relaxing, "I got back from Los Angeles and called up Bob Carlton to see if he'd scheduled the operation and uh, he said he hadn't heard a thing from you guys."

I couldn't say anything. My throat felt full of cotton.

"I decided not to get it," said Jerry, his face twitching nervously.

"May I ask why?" said Alvin, frowning.

"Well," said Jerry, "I just felt like . . ." He looked down at his hands. I guess it's pretty hard to say no to a dream in the flesh.

"Don't want any charity, huh?" says Alvin, quickly filling in the silence. "Now, I thought I made it clear to Roary that this was a loan, not a giveaway. Didn't I make that clear, Roary?"

"That's what Roary told me, but that's not it," said Jerry, sounding frantic.

"Or maybe you figured it was just a fantasy," says Alvin, giving Jerry a questioning look.

"Well, yeah," says Jerry. "It is, isn't it?"

"Man," says Alvin, laughing a little, "what isn't? You know? I mean, what the hell isn't? You think *any* of this is real? It's all a dream, Jerry. You know that, don't you?" He shakes his head and smiles sadly at Jerry. "Look man, I ain't gonna rap to you. I'm just gonna say I think you oughta do it. Dr. Carlton is a good man. He says you could be walking right in five or six months if he operates right now. That means you'll miss next season, but you'll be ready to go the year after that." He reaches out and slaps Jerry's knee. "Man, I know you're good enough for semipro ball. Could you dig that? And who knows, a hot-shot little white guy. If you can pass like you can shoot you might go all the way. Sure it's unreal Jerry, but that's what makes it so good."

Jerry is red as a beet. He doesn't say anything. What can he say when Alvin Martin tells him he's gonna be playing professional basketball in a year? I can't say anything either. I think both of us were just waiting for Alvin to vanish in a puff of smoke and suddenly we'd wake up and everything would be like it always was. But there he was, really, and he didn't seem to be in any hurry to go anywhere.

"Now," says Alvin, suddenly businesslike, "I've asked Dr. Carlton to perform the operation at Stanford Hospital, and then I figured you could stay in the guest house at my place for a while since you'll be going to the hospital every day for therapy and we're just ten minutes from there. That way, when you start walking again I can help you get back in shape and we'll save a lot of money and time."

Jerry shook his head and said "No" very quietly. His face was blank.

"What are you afraid of?" asked Alvin. "You're not afraid of the operation, are you?"

"I don't even know you," said Jerry. "You might hate me."

"No," said Alvin, stretching out his arms towards the ceiling, "I liked you the minute we started to play that day."

"Why?" said Jerry.

"I don't know," says Alvin, shrugging his shoulders and turning to me. "Why does anybody like anybody? Look, if it bothers you, have the operation up here, stay close to your friends, but you gotta take the chance. That's the whole point."

"But why do you want to do this?" asked Jerry, the color starting to come back into his cheeks.

"Because I'm curious."

"About what?" asks Jerry, getting curious himself.

"Oh," says Alvin, grinning, "lots of things. Curious to see if you can beat me again. Curious to see if you can make it in the pros. Curious to see you play. Curious to see if the operation works. All that stuff." He talks so calmly, so sure of himself.

"And what if it doesn't work out?" says Jerry.

"Dr. Carlton says there's no way it can hurt," said Alvin. "Only way you lose is if you don't try."

"I can be happy without it," says Jerry. But he doesn't believe that any more. Hearing it from me he could handle. Hearing it from Alvin is wiping out all that reality crap he handed me.

"Well," says Alvin, laughing a little, "somehow I don't quite believe that, Jerry. As my master says, Your face tells me another story. Your face tells me you're ready to go."

Jerry laughs and Alvin laughs, and I feel like Jerry has just stepped into another world.

26

Bert made it back in time for Jerry's going-away party. We had free beer that night and Jackie Norberg left his spot in front of Woolworth's for the evening to play his accordion for us. Jackson and Bert had an arm-wrestling match. Bert won left-handed, Jackson won right. Max actually left his seat by the cash register and sat at the poker table with Stinky, Blue, Wings and me. Max's was filled to bursting with Jerry's friends. There were at least a hundred guys there who considered Jerry their best friend. It was really something.

Nobody in Max's was much on speechmaking except Jackson, but he stayed out of the spotlight because it was Jerry's party. About eight o'clock, Edith brought out a German chocolate cake she'd made and gave Jerry a big kiss as she set it in front of him. Everybody cheered. It was bizarre. Nobody was sure what we were celebrating. Jerry was going away to be operated on, that's all anybody knew, but it wasn't really a going-away party because he was only going thirty miles south and we all expected to see him again pretty soon. Anyway, a bunch of us had pitched in and gotten a basketball jersey custom made for him. It said MAX's on the front, MAXWELL on the back surrounding the number one of course.

Alvin was sending somebody to pick Jerry up at about nine o'clock that night. Jerry was all packed and ready to go. His suitcase was sitting by the front door. He was wearing a new suit for the occasion. He looked pretty sharp. About eight-thirty he gave a little speech.

"Thanks for the party," he said. "You know, I never went away to college or to the Army, so this is my big chance to experience homesickness." Everybody laughed. It wasn't funny, but in a tense situation people will laugh at anything. "I'm gonna be back in a month or so, and when I can I'll be back here permanently. This is my home and you guys are my family, and I love you. So while I'm gone, don't give Bert or Jackson or Max or Roary a hard time, but give Edith a hard time because she loves it."

"Don't try it," says Edith, putting her hands on her hips.

"Oh go ahead," says Jackson, reaching out and pinching her on the butt.

The place cracked up. Then Jerry picked up his suitcase and went outside to wait for his ride, and everybody who could went out with him and we all stood around in the fog making stupid jokes.

A few minutes later this brown Mercedes pulls up and a young Japanese man gets out, loads Jerry's suitcase in the trunk, Jerry climbs in the front seat and away he goes. I looked around at all the guys waving goodbye to Jerry and it really gets me. I guess Jerry couldn't see us or maybe he was too excited, but he didn't wave back.

Then we all went back inside and finished Edith's cake and sat around not really knowing what to do. Goodbyes are hardest for the people who stay behind, I think, because they don't get all the new sights and experiences to fill in the void. Luckily for us, the Jackson and Edith show got going pretty good and that took our minds off Jerry going away.

27

I was going to take a vacation, go to Lake Tahoe and do some gambling. I wanted to get away from Max's for a while. The place depressed me a little. I thought I'd go visit Jerry after his operation and then get on the bus to Tahoe. He was supposed to be operated on three days after the goodbye party, but the morning of the second day after, I got a call from him. He sounded upset and said he wanted me to come down to Alvin's.

So I went down on the Greyhound to Palo Alto and took a cab out to Alvin's. Jerry was waiting for me at the entrance to the private drive that led up to the house. He got in the cab and told the cabby to take us back to downtown Palo Alto. He looked pale, like he hadn't been sleeping. He was acting very mysteriously and he wouldn't tell me anything until we got out of the cab. He told the cabby to take us to a park, someplace quiet.

So the cabby takes us to a nice little park and we find a bench in the sun and the minute we sit down Jerry blurts out, "I need you to come to the hospital with me."

"You couldn't tell me that over the phone?" I asked, a little peeved at him.

"I wanted to ask you in person," he said. His eyes were a little wild and he seemed really tense.

"You mean once you got me down here," I said snidely.

"Look, Roary," he said, looking away from me, "I need you."

"Aw Jesus, Jerry," I said, feeling sort of used, "what the hell do you need me for?"

"I don't know," he says, staring down at the ground. "I'm scared, Roary, and I need you to be there."

I think for a minute but I can't figure it out, so I say, "When do you go in?"

"This afternoon," he said. "Can you be there?"

"I thought you wanted me to go with you?" I said.

"Well," he says, agitated, "Alvin's driving me there. I thought maybe you could meet us there, like it was a surprise."

"I don't get it," I said. I got it of course. He was ashamed to let Alvin know he needed me.

"I just think it would be better," he said, clearing his throat.

"Okay," I said, "I'll be there. Then what? Where do I stay? How many days do you want me to be around?"

"Just until I leave the hospital, Roary. That's in like three days." He couldn't look me in the eye. "Maybe you could get a motel room."

I'm thinking, Sure, Jerry, make it look like I'm the loyal, slightly dumb friend, tagging along after my hero. Make it look like I came because *I* can't do without *you*, so Alvin doesn't see what a phony you are. I feel hurt, almost an actual pain in my chest. But I realize how scared Jerry is, how he's been thrown into this impossible situation and it's taking everything he's got to keep him from flipping out totally. So I say sure, I'll get a motel room. What difference does it make to me?

Jerry gets a cab back to Alvin's and I get a cab and ask the guy to take me to a cheap motel. He takes me to a place called the Busy Bee Motel, ten dollars a night. It's right on the El Camino Real so it's fairly noisy, but it's not bad. I lie down for a couple hours, watch a little television, and then I get another cab and go over to Stanford Hospital.

It's a pretty fancy hospital with fountains all over the place and beautiful gardens, inner courtyards, sculptures, very classy. I find out from the receptionist that Jerry has just checked in. I wander through the place, buy a couple candy bars in the main lobby and then I go up to Jerry's room on the second floor. I go in and there's Jerry sitting up in bed with Alvin and Alvin's wife, Ellen, sitting on the foot of the bed, talking to him.

"Hey, Roary!" says Jerry, breaking into a big smile. "What a surprise."

"Yeah," I say, but I'm a lousy actor.

"Hello, Roary," says Alvin, getting up to shake my hand. "This is my wife Ellen."

Ellen smiled at me, though I could tell she was freaked a little by me. She's one of the prettiest women I've ever seen.

"Well," I said, trying to sound casual, "I was on my way to

96

Lake Tahoe and then I thought I ought to make sure Jerry was okay before I went off."

"You need a place to stay tonight?" asks Alvin.

"No, thanks. I got a cousin in Palo Alto I'm staying with," I said, wishing like crazy I could go and stay at Alvin's.

We talked for a while more and then Alvin and Ellen left. When he was sure they were gone and couldn't hear us, Jerry said quietly, "Thanks, Roary."

"Forget it," I said.

"You're my best friend," he said.

Then Dr. Carlton came in to examine Jerry. He remembered me but he didn't remember my name. I went out in the hall to get out of his way. "Don't leave," says Jerry.

"I'm right here," I said, leaning against the wall in the corridor, feeling very tired.

After the examination Jerry and I played cards for a while, but then Jerry went to sleep. The doctor had given him some muscle relaxants and a sleeping pill. So I went back to the motel, picked up a couple six packs of beer on the way and watched television until I feel asleep. I had a weird dream that night about being in a space capsule in outer space. I was completely alone. In the dream I thought I was going to be alone forever, which sort of made it a nightmare.

The next morning I went back to the hospital but I was twenty minutes late. They'd already started operating. So I hung around in the lobby reading magazines, watching girls and eating junk for about four hours. This cute little boy who was just learning to walk wandered over to me and started playing with my shoe. I love little kids but I learned a long time ago not to touch them. I just froze and let the kid play with my shoe until his mother rushed over and got him. They take one look at me and they think I'm a deviate. I don't blame them. If I had a kid I'd probably do the same thing. I would just have a different definition for what looks like a deviate.

A couple hours after the operation was over I went up to see Jerry. They'd only used a local anesthetic, numbing him below the waist, but Dr. Carlton had tranquilized him pretty good so he was only barely awake when I walked in. They had just brought him back from the recovery room and he looked pretty terrible, very washed out and dazed.

"Hey, Roary," he says weakly. He smiles at me and reaches out his hand towards me. I take his hand and he holds onto me tightly. "Hey, Roary," he says again, grinning like an idiot.

Alvin came in a few minutes later with Dr. Carlton. They were smiling. "Hi, Roary," says Alvin, putting a hand on my shoulder.

"Hey Alvin," I say.

"Hey man, call me Al," he says. He seems suddenly very young, acting his age for once.

Jerry smiles up at us. "I feel like I'm floating," he says.

"That should wear off in a few hours," says Dr. Carlton, feeling Jerry's forehead. "You'll be happy to know, Jerry, that the operation was tremendously successful, if I do say so myself. It might be necessary to perform another minor operation in a few months, though with proper therapy and a little luck and lots of hard work, that shouldn't be necessary. Everything is lined up perfectly now, it just needs a little time to heal and then you can get to work building those muscles up."

"Thank you," said Jerry, his eyes closing.

"Hey Jerry," said Alvin, "it won't be long before we're working out together."

"Okay," said Jerry. He nods off again and we all tiptoe out.

I stuck around for two days until they moved Jerry to Alvin's house. Then I went up to Lake Tahoe and got a motel room and spent most of my time gambling, though I did rent a motorboat one day and zoom around the lake. It's so beautiful and clean there, I love the smell of pine trees, and driving a boat fast like that is a pretty big physical thrill for me.

Stinky had given me ten dollars to gamble for him, Wings had given me five, and Edith had given me two. I actually came out about sixty dollars ahead. I started feeling lonely after about a week, and since I was nearly out of my own money I went home. But Max's without Jerry takes some getting used to. It took me a long time, another trip to Tahoe a few weeks later and one all the way to Tiajuana with Jackson to get his car reupholstered, before I started feeling like the hole Jerry left was finally filling up.

28

I made a vow that I wasn't going to call Jerry. He had to call me. Maybe that was stupid but I felt like he owed it to me. So August, September, October, November go by and it's almost Christmas. Nothing, not a peep.

I figure he's too busy with his rehabilitation. Dr. Carlton told me Jerry should be walking without crutches within two to three months. So I figure maybe he's waiting until he can walk into Max's and surprise us before he comes. I had Alvin's phone number. I knew I could call Jerry anytime I wanted but I wouldn't let myself.

In the meantime, Max's is rolling right along. We got a waitress, a cousin of Jackson's, but she quits after three weeks because she can't make enough tips and the place is too weird. Then we try out Edith's niece and she quits after three days and tried to take Edith with her. She told Edith she was crazy to want to work in a freak joint. Edith said to her, "Freaks, huh? You ever tried the Holiday Inn?" Then we tried two different girls from the Aquatic Club and they last a total of a month, and then finally we find Louise, who is perfect and absolutely beautiful except she has one leg shrunken from polio which makes her limp a little. She fits like she was born in Max's.

Louise has reddish-brown hair, wavy, and it comes down just below her shoulders. She's tall, almost my height, five foot nine, and though some guys think she's skinny, I think she's perfect. For some reason she seems sort of Irish to me. She's an actress and tends to be fairly dramatic even when she's not onstage.

Of course everyone, including me, falls madly in love with her. Inside a month she's had four marriage proposals and she gets boxes of candy like every day is Valentine's Day. I give her a rose every once in a while, but I make sure I give Edith one too. Louise handles it all beautifully. She tells everyone that she'll make up her mind who she'll marry when she turns thirty. That's three years away.

I just knew Jerry would flip over her too and that she would love him but I can't even get a postcard from him, let alone set him up.

Everybody was getting in a Christmasy mood, most of the vets were starting to hang out at the veteran's hospital to pick up on the charity presents, Edith brought in mistletoe and hung it all over the place, and every once in a while Louise would kiss some lucky bastard and the place would go wild. But here I was preoccupied with Jerry again. I resented him so much I couldn't stand it. The bastard owed me a letter, if not a phone call, if there was some good reason he didn't come in person. So in early December I sent him a letter. Here it is.

Dear Jerry,
    In case you've forgotten, my name is Roary. I used to be your best friend, or so you said. I'm sure you're working very hard and you're very busy but I sure would appreciate hearing from

you, hearing about your recuperation and how life is treating you.

Jason Watson got hit by a car and broke his leg. He got 12,000 dollars for it. Stinky says hello, so does Wings. Stinky has a girlfriend named Claire. She looks sort of like Shirley Temple. She's short, cute, has curly hair and is sort of old fashioned looking. She comes in sometimes and sits with us but I think mainly she and Stinky have a good thing going sexually. Don't laugh, I think it's true.

Wings won 75 dollars at Bay Meadows the other day. Bet on a horse named Chunky if you can believe it. Blue says he'll wait to say hello until you show up in person. Bert got in a fight about six weeks ago with some guy in Chinatown. Bert broke two fingers. The guy apparently mistook Bert for some guy who had been fooling with his wife. Bert said, "I wouldn't even know what to do with a Chinese woman." Jackson says, "You do exactly the same thing with a Chinese woman that you do with a Japanese woman, only you reverse the angle." Bad jokes as usual.

And we got a gorgeous waitress named Louise who is too good for mere words to describe. You'd fall in love with her in a minute but she's too good for you. Oh yeah and I had a good time at Lake Tahoe, twice! Jackson and I went to Tiajuana and saw a really lousy bullfight. They had this old cow that could hardly walk. The guy comes out, stabs it. Big deal.

Say, why don't you come visit? Alvin comes up this way to practice anyway, doesn't he?

So, whatever,

Love,
Roary

I kept it friendly.

Basketball season had started up, the preseason games anyway, and Alvin was back in the sports headlines again, scoring thirty-five points a game. The Warriors are favored to win their division again. I kept waiting for a human interest story to come out about Alvin helping Jerry, but I guess they were

101

waiting to write that *after* they saw whether Jerry panned out or not.

Then all of a sudden it was Christmas. We had a big party at Max's. Edith cooked six turkeys and about forty pumpkin pies. "Some retirement," she shouted when Jackson toasted her on Christmas Eve. We set up a microphone in front of the big video screen and Jackson did about an hour routine that left everybody on the floor. And then Louise got up and led us through some Christmas carols. It was nice and sappy, but it was spoiled for me because Jerry hadn't written.

Then three days *after* Christmas a package arrives at Max's addressed to me. I usually get my mail at my apartment, but I can tell by the handwriting this is from Jerry. Naturally Jackson and Bert crowd around as I open it. There's a letter which I put in my pocket for later. The box is full of presents for all the guys, each one is labeled. There's even one for Louise.

"Good old Jerry," says Bert.

"Yeah?" I say. "Well, why couldn't he bring this himself, *before* Christmas? The sucker's only thirty miles away!"

"Oh give him a break," says Bert. Bert doesn't understand why I'm upset. Bert has infinite patience, too much patience I think sometimes.

Jackson got a wallet, Bert got a bottle of scotch, Edith got some perfume, Louise got a lovely embroidered handkerchief she said she was going to frame, Max got a photograph of Los Angeles in 1920, and everybody else got either a deck of cards or a portable checkers set, except Stinky, who got a Braille copy of *Lady Chatterley's Lover*. I got a three-year subscription to *Sports Illustrated* and a ten-dollar gift certificate to Blum's Candies, which used to be my favorite store.

The letter, which I read later, said

Dear Roary,

Please dispense all these gifts for me. I would have come myself but I have been working very hard and I really haven't

102

had any time. I get up at 6:30, do yoga stretching for an hour, eat breakfast, swim for an hour, go to the hospital for three hours of physical therapy, come home, eat lunch, rest for an hour, take a walk (I've worked up to an hour, trying for two), swim for another hour, then I get a massage and heat treatment, rest for half an hour, eat dinner, talk or read for a while and then GO TO BED!

On weekends it's much the same only I sleep more on Sunday instead of going to the hospital. The trick is to work as hard as I can without hurting myself. Sometimes I'm so worn out I fall asleep without dinner. Even so, I should have written or at least called. I have no excuse except I guess I was raised wrong. I promise to come visit as soon as I can, like January 15th?

Alvin isn't around much, but when he is he works out with me. He and Ellen are terrific people, though he can really get distant in a hurry. So many people are constantly bugging him. Ellen is a dancer in a modern dance group in Palo Alto and she teaches dance too. They both wear their wealth pretty well. They aren't snobs about it.

Joseph, the man who drove me from Max's, is a second-degree black belt of the same school of Karate that Alvin studies. He instructs Alvin in between lessons with their master, Shiro Ishigawa, who's in Japan most of the time. Alvin is a third-degree brown belt.

This place is really fantastic. They've got a beautiful pool which I practically live in it seems, and a gymnasium that looks like a pagoda from the outside. The Japanese woman you met is Joseph's wife. She and Joseph both attend Stanford University. Joe is a chemist and Miyoshi is a dietitian, and man can she cook! But mostly I have the place pretty much to myself.

Well, the eyelids are drooping. Thanks for being so patient with crazy Jerry.

Love,
Jerry

So it made sense why he hadn't written or called, I thought. And he was coming to visit. I was really excited about seeing him again. I tried to imagine him walking into Max's without a limp, but I couldn't.

I wrote him back telling him how happy I was he was coming. I told him the guys were all dying to see him and if he wanted to we could have a homecoming party. But he never wrote back, so I forgot the party idea.

29

January 2. I went on my first date since I was in the Army. I found out from Edith that Louise was crazy for ballet. So I got two tickets to the San Francisco Ballet and asked her to go. She practically fainted. I was in great spirits since Jerry had written and I just felt like celebrating. I took Louise out to dinner to this really good Armenian restaurant.

Louise is so beautiful that when I sit at a table with her I forget she has one skinny leg. I know I'm way out of my league, but if I can have her to myself for a whole evening just for the price of two ballet tickets, I'll get season tickets, hell I'll become a patron.

So we eat and then we go to the ballet. It was really good. The music was terrific. It was the first live orchestra music I'd ever heard except for our high school orchestra which was awful, especially the violins. These violins, the ones at the ballet, were perfect. The ballet was *Giselle* and the people in it were all terrific, especially this one Russian guy that just flew all over the place, jumping about six feet in the air. I wondered if he'd ever tried playing basketball.

Afterwards Louise invited me over to her place and we talked about the ballet and about our lives. She told me about the time she almost killed herself because she couldn't dance. She married a guy when she was nineteen but she didn't love him she said. They got divorced after a year and then she went to acting school for two years in Los Angeles and then she started waitressing and trying out for plays. She'd had some small parts but never anything big.

She was still trying out for parts whenever she could but she hadn't gotten anything in over a year. I was thinking that it was probably because of her leg, because she was perfect otherwise, but she read my mind. "It's not because of my leg either," she said. "It's because it takes a while to make the right connections and then the right part has to come along. It'll happen one of these days."

"Maybe you should write your own play," I said.

"Maybe so," she said, messing up my hair on her way to get coffee, "or maybe you could write it for me."

I laughed at that. The thought of me writing anything seemed ridiculous. I didn't have the intellectual development, let alone any ideas. But I had some great fantasies about writing a play for her, some knockout smash hit and leaving it anonymously in her mailbox.

30

January 15th finally came. I didn't think it ever would, the days were going so slow. It was raining like crazy and Max's was jammed because everybody knew Jerry was coming to visit. I didn't know exactly what time, that was the only problem. We made a sign on butcher paper about five feet long that said WELCOME HOME JERRY and we taped it so it hung down in front of the bar.

People were getting pretty restless by four o'clock, myself included. Louise had to leave for a tryout, she'd already stayed an extra hour to meet him, and Edith was getting ready to go too. I just wished he'd told me what time he was coming. Finally, just before five, I get a phone call from Jerry.

He's at Ghirardelli Square, can I meet him there he wants to know.

"Jerry," I say, whispering into the phone, "the guys are all waiting to see you."

"Jees, Roary, I'm sorry," he says. His voice sounds different. "I've only got an hour and I thought we could eat here."

So I explain to the guys that Jerry got tied up unexpectedly. You can tell they're disappointed.

I hurry out into the rain and just catch the Judah down to Market Street and then I grab the cable car over to Ghirardelli. When it's raining the cable car isn't usually crowded and it's pretty fast going over to the waterfront. I'm so excited about seeing him I can't even stay mad at him for not coming to Max's. All the way down I'm trying to imagine him walking without a limp, so that when I really see him I won't be too surprised, but I just can't do it.

I get off the cable car and I'm on my way into Ghirardelli Square when suddenly I see him coming. He's not limping. He looks about six inches taller and he's so graceful. I can't believe it.

He sees me and waves, then he spins around and walks backwards, then spins back around and actually runs a little. "Hey, Roary!" he says, shaking my hand and smiling. We're both getting soaked. "Boy, it's good to see you," he says, hugging me.

"Christ, Jerry," I say, "you look terrific! You look like you've gained twenty pounds!" He looked so healthy and strong I couldn't get over it.

"You look terrific too, Roary," he said, though I know I looked the same as always. "Let's get out of the rain."

So we go for some sandwiches in a little cafe, find a table and sit down to talk. All I could really think to say was how great he looked, but when I took a bite of my sandwich I wanted to ask him why he didn't come to Max's. We have much better sandwiches and we're just as close to Palo Alto, but I'm afraid to ask.

"So how are you, Roary?" he says.

"Well, fine," I say, feeling like I'm reading lines or something. It all feels very unnatural. "I sold part of my share of Max's to Bert and I told you about Louise. Well, she and I go to the ballet now." I didn't know what else to say. A short silence fell.

"That's terrific," he says, filling in quickly. "I went to the ballet with Alvin and Ellen just the other night. Ellen's a dancer."

"Yeah, you said that in your letter," I said.

"Really, Roary," he says, smiling steadily, "I told you everything pretty much. I just work out and sleep and eat. I can't relax. It's like I'm hurrying to get out of there and stop depending on Alvin."

"What does the doctor say?" I ask.

"Oh, he's amazed," said Jerry, nodding confidently. "He says I for sure won't need another operation. I'm months ahead of where he thought I'd be. He said I can start running and jumping anytime now. I've already started shooting again. Boy, it's weird, everything feels so different."

"So when do you think you'll be moving out of there?" I asked.

"A month, maybe six weeks."

"And then where?"

"Well," says Jerry, "I'm gonna try out for the team."

"The Warriors?" I said.

"Well, the farm team," he said, grinning at me. "You know like if they like me well enough they'll get me on a semipro team where they can keep an eye on me. That's what Alvin says anyway."

"This year?" I said. I was totally amazed.

"Yeah," said Jerry. "And then next year I can try out again and if I'm good enough . . ."

"Jerry," I said, "that's fantastic! That's incredible!" I was so excited I couldn't sit still.

"Yeah," he said, turning red. "*If* they like me."

"Aw Jerry," I said, "how could they not?"

"I gotta work, Roary," he said, getting very serious. "I won't be anywhere near my full potential by the time I try out. I can walk fine now but I can hardly run or jump at all. In six weeks I'll be just getting started, and when I try out in March, I'll only be a little further along. I really need another six months of hard work."

"So you probably won't be moving back to Frisco," I said. I don't know what that had to do with anything but it just popped out.

"Not for a while," he said.

"Not for a year at least," I said.

"Oh I don't know," he said, looking away, his mind somewhere else.

"Hey Jerry," I said, "you oughta come visit. The guys would love to see you and I want you to meet Louise."

"I've been meaning to, Roary," he says, "but I really want to have a whole day, so they don't think I'm just breezing through."

"Aw Jerry, they'd be happy with five minutes. Please drop by."

"Okay, Roary," he says. "Next chance I get."

It had stopped raining so we walked around Ghirardelli for another fifteen minutes, looking in the windows of the fancy shops, and then we went to wait on the sidewalk for Ellen to come. She arrives a few minutes later in a white Mercedes, waves to me, Jerry shakes my hand and says he'll write and then off they go. And then it starts to rain again.

Now the whole time we were talking I could tell Jerry was afraid to go back to Max's. I think he was afraid something there would rub off on him again, that his leg would go bad and his dream would be over. And I could understand that, because he wasn't crippled any more, but goddamnit he was still Jerry and he owed us something, me and every guy in Max's.

The more I thought about it the more pissed off I got. I

wanted to scream or hit somebody. I started walking across town, back to Max's, and after about ten blocks I calm down enough to try and put myself in Jerry's place. My back is healed, I can run and jump and they want me to play professional football. Can I still hang out at Max's? I think I can because I'm one of the guys, I interact with them. But Jerry, except when he was really depressed, never really hung out there. He worked there and he would never call himself a cripple. There really was a difference. He had never really joined the club. He was holding out for the miracle all that time. The rest of us would take a miracle if it came along, but we weren't waiting for it. I wasn't anyway. I guess I was waiting for other sorts of things, but my body I had no illusions about.

31

Well, Jerry didn't write and I finally wrote him at the beginning of March, just a postcard, asking him to come to Max's. He called me when he got the card and said he was sorry he hadn't written but he was getting ready for the tryout that was in less than two weeks and as soon as it was over he was going to definitely come to Max's. I guess I was pretty hard on him. I told him I was having a hard time believing him since he kept saying he would do things and then he didn't.

He promised he'd come to Max's at the end of March at the latest. I asked him the date and time but he didn't know. He'd check and call me back in a couple days, he said. "I'm counting on you to call, Jerry," I said. "I'm waiting for your call."

"Okay," he said.

Now I don't know, maybe he got off the phone and said,

"Jesus, I wish Roary would stop bugging me." But I don't care.

I had tickets to another ballet for that night. Louise had been trying out for plays and acting companies and television commercials all week *and* working four hours a day at Max's, so she's pretty tired and a little depressed. But you say the word "ballet" to her and it's like somebody has shot her full of adrenalin.

We eat at Lefty O'Doul's, a restaurant with pictures of baseball players all over the walls. It's a nice place, smorgasbord style and pretty cheap compared to some of the places in town. I guess I was pretty preoccupied with Jerry again because I kept daydreaming all through dinner.

"You're weird tonight," says Louise as we're leaving the joint.

"Oh I'm just pissed off at Jerry," I said.

She laughed a little. "Sometimes I wonder if he really exists," she said. "I've heard so much about him but I've never seen him. He's like a god at Max's, but seriously, Roary, sometimes I think he must be some sort of group illusion."

That cracked me up, because that's sure what he'd become. I realized how much I talked about him as if he was there, as if Louise knew him as well as I did. But really he *was* just an illusion now.

Then that night at the ballet I see him. Louise and I were in the first balcony and before the ballet starts I'm looking around at the people and then I see Jerry coming down the aisle in the orchestra section below us. He's with a woman, a stunning blonde in a slinky black dress. He's wearing a black tuxedo and looks like a goddamn movie star. The woman he's with looks like a movie star too. My heart is pounding like crazy. Then Alvin and Ellen come down the aisle and they all sit together in the fourth row center, talking and laughing, and I can see Jerry has them all just cracking up, loving him. Christ, no wonder he's having a hard time coming back to Max's.

"What's the matter?" says Louise, "you look positively shocked."

"I just saw Jerry," I said, but the lights went out before I could point him out to her and she accused me of hallucinating.

I could hardly watch the ballet. I kept trying to see Jerry and how he was reacting to the dancing. I couldn't get over how he looked, how suave he was. Nobody at Max's would believe it.

The ballet was good again. The violins were perfect as usual and the Russian guy jumped around beautifully again. I especially wanted to see how Jerry liked that part. I wondered if Jerry was thinking about the guy trying to play basketball too.

At intermission I pointed Jerry out to Louise. "That's Jerry?" she said, looking through the opera glasses. "Wow, is he ever handsome!"

"Yeah," I said, "he's a real cutie pie."

"Well, let's go see him," she said, raising her eyebrows at me. "Let's go mingle with the chosen people."

"Naw, I don't want to bother him," I said. Bother him my ass, I didn't want to ruin him in front of that woman.

"I thought he was your best friend," said Louise, pouting. "Come on, let's go see him." She pulled my arm, teasing me.

"No," I said, feeling myself about to scream at her.

"Why not?" she asks, giving me this disgruntled look.

"Because," I said.

"It's ridiculous," she said, waving her arms around dramatically, "you gripe all day long about never getting to see him and here he is in the same building! I seriously doubt if that *is* Jerry, if there even *is* a Jerry."

"You go see him, then," I said. "You go up to him and say, 'Hello, Jerry, my name is Louise. I'm a friend of Roary's.' You see if he doesn't know me."

"Okay," she said, standing up, "I will."

"No, don't!" I said.

"Then, you do it," she said, looking down at me defiantly.

"I can't," I said.

"Okay then, here I go," she said, and off she went.

I figured Louise was so pretty it wouldn't hurt Jerry's image if she went up to him. But if I went up to him, forget it. Even so, I kept glancing around nervously, afraid Jerry might feel obligated to come say hello.

Louise was gone a long time. She made it back just as Act Two was starting. She was out of breath from hurrying. "I take it back," she said, "he certainly does know you. I thanked him for the handkerchief too."

"Oh yeah?" I said. I wanted to know everything, what he said, what the woman looked like up close, everything, but the ballet was on and Louise was transfixed. Then at a break between scenes she leans over and says, "They want to meet us for drinks afterwards."

"No!" I said, "we can't." A bunch of people around us said "Shh!" but I was in a panic.

"Why not, Roary?" she asked. I could hear she really felt hurt.

"I gotta go," I said, getting up. I was suffocating. I had to get out of there.

Louise stayed behind to see the rest of the ballet, and then she found Jerry and company and told them I'd gotten sick and had to leave. Then she came over to my place to find out what was wrong. She said they had all acted very concerned about me and she assured them it was just an upset stomach. She said Jerry was going to call me to see how I was doing.

I told her that I thought Jerry would have been embarrassed to have his date meet me. Louise said it was Jerry who suggested we get together, but I knew Jerry. He knew I wouldn't show. He knew I'd run away first. I told Louise that and she said Jerry certainly sounded sincere to her and I said he may have seemed sincere but he was just a good actor. I didn't mind, though, I wanted to get off that subject and find out more about how Jerry was, what his date was like, stuff like that.

"You're crazy," said Louise. "One minute you're running away like they're gonna devour you and the next minute you want to hear all about them. What's your problem, Roary?"

I can't explain it to her. How can I explain that it's not *my* problem, it's Jerry's problem and I'm just looking out for him? I think for a minute and then I say, "Because Jerry's been ashamed of me before, the way I look and stuff."

"Are you ashamed of the way you look?" she asks.

"Yeah," I say, "around fancy people I am."

"You'd rather be nice-looking, right?" she says.

"Aw cut it out, Louise," I tell her.

"Seriously," she says, "if you care so much, why don't you shave, get a haircut and lose some weight?"

"I've got scars," I say, "and besides I don't care because I don't choose to be around fancy people." I don't know why I was calling them fancy people. It was a stupid expression.

"Big deal," she says, "you like being ugly. It's your crutch."

"Go to hell," I say.

"Well, don't blame Jerry," she says.

"You don't know shit about Jerry," I said, getting mad.

"I know he was waiting to see you, to go out with us," she said, scowling at me.

"He knew I'd leave," I told her again.

"Oh I see," she said, "he hates you so much he went out of his way to invite us for drinks because he knew you'd leave. Really, Roary, would your best friend do that? I mean, why would he bother inviting us for drinks?"

"Are you sure *he* invited us?" I asked, "and not Alvin."

"I didn't speak to Alvin," she said, "just Jerry. He was about to come up to say hi to you when they blinked the lights."

I felt a little dumb, but I didn't regret not staying. The way I looked, it would have ruined everything.

"Now," said Louise, "how about I shave you and give you a haircut?"

"Go to hell," I said, but I said it friendly because I knew she was just teasing me.

"Please," she said, pouting her lips. Then she smiled. "You could be just as handsome as Jerry if you wanted to."

"Bullshit," I said.

"You could, Roary. Underneath all that hair is a very good-looking man."

"With scars," I said.

Then she came close and lifted my whiskers here and there. "Two little ones," she said. "Big deal." Louise loves to say "big deal."

"Believe me," I said, "I look terrible."

"I don't believe you," she said. "I believe you're a handsome man who's hiding from the world. I can see it in your eyes."

"What can you see?" I said, "that I'm hiding or that I'm handsome?"

"Both," she said.

"Quit projecting," I said. I didn't really mean that, but I felt cornered and saying "quit projecting" is a good defense tactic Jerry taught me.

She looked at me very seriously. "I wouldn't say all this if I didn't care about you, Roary. I hope you know that."

"I know that," I said. She was right of course, everything she said was right, but knowing someone is right and doing something about it are always two different things.

"So why don't you shave and get a haircut," she said, poking me in the ribs.

"Go to hell," I said.

"You already said that," she said. She was teasing me.

And then it hit me, this was making love for us. Until I could let that other me out, this was all there would ever be for me in terms of loving Louise. A nice evening on the town and teasing.

Anyway, I decided to go on a diet, see how it went, and at least trim my beard a little.

32

In the middle of March, Jerry spent a day scrimmaging with the Warriors. Alvin set it up for him. He called me afterwards to tell me he'd done well enough to get put on a semipro team based in San Jose, part of the West Coast Athletic League. He wasn't going to start but he was definitely going to play. He was going to play in his first game that week! He wondered if I could make it.

"I'll be there, Jerry!" I shouted, "if you'll promise to come to Max's afterwards and see the guys."

"Okay," he said, "it's a deal."

"You gotta promise," I said.

"Okay, okay, I promise," he says. "The game is at eight o'clock Thursday night in San Jose. We're playing at San Jose State, so I'll have a college career after all."

"You better play good, Jerry," I say, teasing him. "I been bragging about you."

"Listen, Roary," he says, sounding pretty tired, "I'll be happy just to play."

So Thursday night Jackson and I drive down to San Jose. So what if it was just a little semipro game, Jerry was gonna be playing, actually playing. I was so excited I couldn't wait to get there. I kept telling Jackson to drive faster, even though he was already speeding. He pretended I was insane and kept giving me this fearful look and muttering under his breath about the master turning into a maniac. I did feel kind of wild, like I was gonna be playing or something. Plus I was excited he was actually going to come back to Max's.

In case you didn't know it, semipro basketball is not really a transition between college and pro ball. It's not like the baseball farm system at all. It's a weird bunch of leagues, some very well organized, others fairly loosely put together. Semipro basketball is full of guys on their way down, a few on their way up, and several people who can't play ball at all but are big and strong and mean. It's about the roughest basketball you'll ever see, brutal even. There's more physical contact than in most football games, and just as many injuries. I know because I'd gone to some games with Jerry and, compared to pro ball, semipro was Rugby and pro ball was ballet.

Also, there aren't very many small white guys in semipro ball in California. In fact, there aren't many white guys in it at all. Jerry always used to say that if he ever had to play semipro he'd try to get tight with the biggest black guy on his team, and hide behind him.

Too bad the Warriors were on the road, or Alvin might have been there for the game. I wish he had been there because if he'd seen the way they knocked Jerry around, he probably would have gone out on the court and cracked a few heads together.

When Jerry went into the game in the first half I went completely crazy. I was jumping up and down, pounding Jackson on the back, making a fool of myself screaming. I'm sure everybody thought I was a psycho, but I just couldn't help myself. I mean here was Jerry flying down the court, running on his toes. What else could I do under the circumstances?

Unfortunately, my excitement faded after about thirty seconds and turned into violent anger because they were just murdering him out there. You see, Jerry is not only an unbelievable outside shot, he's got some of the most beautiful inside moves you'll ever see. It's a big part of his game and it works so long as people are playing basketball, not butcherball. The first time Jerry drove the lane that night in San Jose he got slugged so hard I thought his jaw was broken at least. No foul was called. Jerry played five minutes of the first half, only touched the ball a few times, and got knocked over so many times I lost count.

"He's just too small to be trading punches with those dudes," said Jackson, shaking his head as the first half was ending.

"He's a basketball player," I said angrily, "not a hockey puck!"

Jackson grinned at me. "He'll figure it out, Roary. He's got it, don't worry about it."

"Okay," I said. "I'm sorry."

I knew what Jerry was going through. He was suffering. Here he was on the edge of a dream and it was turning ugly. The only small guys who ever made it in the pros came up through college, playing in leagues with good referees and fans that wouldn't tolerate brutality on the court. Nobody small had ever come up out of the gutter leagues that I knew about.

There were only a hundred or so people in the gym, the two teams stayed on the court during halftime, shooting baskets, staying loose. They knew there weren't any scouts in the crowd, so it was pretty relaxed. Jerry stayed on the bench, his head bowed. I decided he needed cheering up, so I asked Jackson to go down and say something to him, but Jackson was busy flirting with some girls, so I went.

Jerry was sitting there in a daze, staring at the floor. "How you doing?" I said, walking up to him.

"Roary," he said, snapping out of his trance and smiling up at me. "You made it."

"You got two big fans here, Jer. You hit a basket and Jackson and me'll tear the place apart."

"They won't give me the ball, Roary," he said sadly. "It's not a real clean game either."

"I noticed," I said. "How's your leg?"

"My leg is great. The rest of me is a giant bruise."

"Can't you gun from outside?" I asked.

"Oh I will, Roary, but first I gotta get the damn thing in my hands," he says, starting to get pissed off.

"You will," I said. "You will."

"Okay," he said, shaking his head. "I will."

Jerry didn't start the second half and might not have gotten in at all if Jackson and I hadn't started chanting, "We want Maxwell, we want Maxwell." They put Jerry in with about three minutes left. He finally got a pass from somebody and shot the ball from so far out the crowd groaned, but it turned out the shot wasn't a shot at all, but a pass, right into the hands of the big center on Jerry's team. He rammed the ball through the hoop for an easy two, and then as he ran down the court to play defense, he slapped Jerry's hands.

With about a minute left in the game, Jerry got a pass from his new friend, went up from twenty feet out, arched the ball high over the defender's hands and the ball whistled down through the hoop clean. And that was all it took for the Jerry Maxwell fan club to go totally berserk. As berserk as two people can go in a big nearly-empty gym with a few dozen other people staring at us like we were crazy, which I suppose we were. But so what?

That night at Max's was an incredibly high time. As far as I was concerned the miracle was complete. What more could we possibly ask for? Stinky was so glad to have Jerry back he wouldn't let go of Jerry once he got a hold of him. When he introduced Jerry to his girlfriend Claire and Jerry told Stinky he thought Claire was a real knockout, Stinky just about floated away he was so happy.

Max talked a blue streak, like thirty words. "How are you, Jerry?" he said. "You look great. When you gonna be on the tube? Soon, I hope. Good to see you." That's a blue streak for Max.

Bert wrestled Jerry around some, bawled him out for not coming sooner, made Jerry walk around the room a few times showing off how good his leg was. Everybody applauded. Jackson said, "Here he is, Mr. America." We all laughed but inside we were proud, I'm not sure of what but I know we were.

Anyway, Louise was nuts about Jerry and he seemed to like her pretty well too. She was flirting with him like crazy, laughing at his jokes when they weren't funny, bringing him beer, inviting him with her eyes. She hardly said a word to me all night. I could hardly blame her. He looked terrific. He is terrific. I was jealous, but then again it seemed okay in a way. I loved them both, why shouldn't they love each other?

We stayed up until two in the morning talking and Jerry ended up spending the night in his old room at Max's. In the morning I hopped on the N Judah with him, just like old times, rode down to BART and then took BART with him as far south as Daly City.

He said he was going to stay in the guest house at Alvin's for a while more, but he was looking for an apartment near Stanford. He said he really liked the area. He also asked me lots of questions about Louise. Was I in love with her? I said not really. Did she have a boyfriend? I said no. Would she like to come to a game? I said probably. I could tell he was gonna ask her out and suddenly I felt very resentful. Here he was using me again, not intentionally but that's what was happening. I told him Louise was a wonderful person and that if he really wanted to make a good impression on her he oughta take her to a ballet. I should have just told him to go to hell, but instead I practically gave her away.

33

As it turned out, Jerry didn't have any time to put the moves on Louise. During the next two weeks he played seven games, most of them on the road in Southern California. He called us long distance after the sixth game, which he played in Los

Angeles. He'd finally busted loose and scored nineteen points in front of a big crowd. He was bursting, he said, and just had to tell us about it.

That made me really happy, and then he asked to speak to Louise. I wanted to ask him what for, but it wasn't any of my business so I didn't say anything. She wasn't there anyway, so he said to just tell her he called. I let Bert give her the message.

It sort of bothered me the way he was suddenly so interested in Louise, but then again it sure seemed to make him want to stay in touch with us, and I'd been saying ever since I knew him that what he needed was a good woman, so I decided to quit being an idiot and let things go.

And then on the morning of April 3, I'll never forget that date, Jackson comes running into Max's waving the *Chronicle*. "Hey!" he shouted, "Jerry's gonna be playing for the Warriors! They brought him up to the regular team!"

I remember taking the sports page from Jackson and looking at it. "Where? Where!?" I'm shouting, and Jackson has to point to the exact spot on the page where it said Jerry was being brought up because the Warriors had been weak at the guard spot for several games because of illness and injuries. They were three games out of first place, the season was almost over and they were getting desperate. There's no way to describe how I felt.

So we closed Max's at seven o'clock that night and Bert, Jackson, Louise, Blue, Edith and I all piled into Jackson's car and went over to Oakland to see the game. The game was almost sold out, it was against Portland, so we got terrible seats, but we were there anyway. I've never been so excited in my life. Semipro was one thing, but this was too much.

Jackson kept chanting, "Unbelievable, unbelievable," and Blue kept shaking his head and saying, "Unreal, un*real*," and Edith kept saying, "Little Jerry? Our Jerry?" and Bert bought everybody beer and passed out cigars like he'd just had a baby. But we had to act crazy because it *was* crazy.

The two teams came out and started warming up but we

couldn't spot Jerry. "Oh crap," said Bert, "don't tell me they changed their minds?"

"I don't see Alvin yet either," said Jackson. "They're probably teaching Jerry the rules as fast as they can."

We all laughed at that but I was starting to worry. His name wasn't in the program because they wouldn't have had time to print a new one, but it bugged me anyway. Eventually we spotted Alvin but no Jerry. "Aw shit," I said, squirming in my seat.

"Look," said Louise, sounding like an old lady talking to a little boy, "we're here, we paid, let's enjoy the game."

That was easy for her to say, but I was going crazy. The teams finished warming up and then they went to their benches, we stood for the national anthem and then the announcer introduced the starting teams. After he'd announced the last Warrior starter he said, "And now I'd like to introduce a newcomer to the Warriors, playing in his first NBA contest five foot nine inches tall, from our own San Francisco, won't you please welcome Jerry Maxwell." Then Jerry ran out onto the court, waved, then ran back to the bench. He'd been there all the time, warming up and everything. We just hadn't seen him. He just didn't look anything like Jerry from so far away. It was a real shock.

"Doesn't look like Jerry," said Blue, puzzled. "Maybe it's a different Jerry Maxwell."

Jackson borrowed a pair of binoculars from a woman in front of us and we all took turns looking at Jerry sitting on the bench. It was him all right, we just hadn't recognized him. His hair was much shorter and the fancy white uniform changed him completely.

The Warriors got in trouble early and it seemed like they emptied their entire bench, but still Jerry didn't get in. They were playing forwards at the guard positions, centers at forwards, but no Jerry. Portland was leading by eighteen with about four minutes left in the first half and it looked like a runaway. Then they put in Jerry. I held my breath.

The first thing he did was run into somebody and fall

down. That got a big laugh from the crowd and I felt like screaming, Shut up! Give him a chance! But I just sat there sweating. Nobody gave him the ball and nobody gave the man he was guarding the ball, but it didn't really matter to me because he was out there running and that was enough ten times over.

With two minutes left in the half, Jerry leaves his man and double-teams Portland's other guard. He knifed the ball away from him and set off down the court towards his basket. I'm on my feet screaming. He had the shot but Alvin was trailing and Jerry passed off, Alvin went high and dunked it and the crowd went wild. And then, before we had a chance to calm down from that, Jerry steals the ball again, drives under the basket and flips the ball in backwards over his head. The crowd starts really waking up now.

With a minute and twenty seconds to go in the half, Portland decides to test Jerry. He's only five foot nine and he's guarding a guy six foot four, so they pass to his man and clear out that side of the court leaving Jerry alone with his man. The guy starts to drive towards the basket and Jerry just streaks around him, swats the ball away and starts off down the court with the ball again. This time there's two guys chasing him. He goes up from fifteen feet out and looks like he's gonna shoot and get his shot blocked because Portland's six foot nine forward is right on top of him, but at the last second Jerry floats the ball off to one side and suddenly there's Alvin again, flying in from nowhere, he snatches the pass, takes one step and slam dunks it again. Everybody in the Pavilion is on their feet screaming.

Portland misses their next shot with forty-five seconds left in the half, the Warriors bring the ball downcourt and Jerry gets a pass. He's thirty feet away from the hoop and his man is waiting for him to move closer, but Jerry just lets the ball go out of his hands, it floats up, curves down and swishes through the hoop. The crowd goes totally bananas.

Portland brings the ball down but they're clearly shaken

up. Their lead is suddenly down to eight and going fast and you can tell they're thinking, Who is this guy anyway?

They miss their shot, Duke, the Warrior's center, snags the rebound and fires the ball to Jerry. With ten seconds left, Jerry charges down the court, leaves his man looking foolish at half court and drives right down the middle of the key, right into this forest of giants, all of them flailing their arms around trying to block the shot. But Jerry is leading a charmed life right then, and when he takes off I suddenly have this image of him smiling as he floats inside, cradling the ball in his arms, as he drifts behind Alvin's screen and lets the ball go out of his hands. It hits the glass backboard and drops through the hoop and then the buzzer sounds and the crowd is roaring.

Like Jerry always says, nobody's ever ready for him the first time. Well they weren't ready for him in the second half either. With ten minutes left in the game he came off the bench and stole the ball three more times, had five assists and finished the game with fifteen points. The Warriors won by nine points. We tried to go see him after the game but you couldn't get within fifty yards of the locker room, there were so many people trying to get in there.

On the way home, Jackson kept making jokes about how much Jerry was going to get paid next year, since he was not only white but he was under six feet tall. He said when you find somebody the public can really identify with, then you got a gold mine. It's funny, but I never thought of Jerry making money. I always just thought of him playing.

34

I tried to get in touch with Jerry the next day but the line at
Alvin's was busy the whole day. The green section of the
Chronicle ran the headline WARRIOR SUB STEALS THE SHOW,
and I just sat there in Max's reading it over and over again.
The article mentioned his name four times and said if he
could be consistent the Warriors might have solved their
guard problem.

But just in case Jerry's career turned out to be short-lived,
we all went to the game the next night. Jackson drove a
bunch of people over and about ten of us chipped in and
rented a big van and Bert drove us over. Going on BART
would have been fun, but too many of the guys couldn't really move fast enough and it would have been an awful lot of
trouble, which it was anyway.

We got to the game early to give us time to get everybody
to their seats. I get worn out just getting myself up and down
a hundred steps, but because the game was so nearly sold out
we had to settle for seats scattered all over the place, but it
was worth it. The Warriors were playing the Bucks, who were
on a nine-game winning streak, so it was going to be a great
game, not that it would have made much difference who they
were playing since we had come to see Jerry, but it did make a
difference because Jerry had always been so awestruck by the
Bucks.

I was sitting with Robert Kovacs, who is very nice except
he's blind and keeps asking me to tell him what Jerry is doing,
and Felix Biderke, also a sweet guy, paralyzed on his left side.
His problem is he's from England and wanted me to explain
to him how the game is played, which I tried to do while at

the same time trying to tell Robert Kovacs what Jerry is or isn't doing. I don't think either of them knew what I was talking about. I would rather have sat with Louise or Bert, but we decided to scatter ourselves to take care of the guys who needed the most help.

Finally the game started, Jerry on the bench. Alvin was just sensational. Midway through the first quarter it looked like the Bucks were going to lose by fifty points, but then the Warriors got cold, the Bucks got hot and it was all tied at the half, but still no Jerry. So in the second half I started secretly rooting for the Bucks just so the guys would get a chance to see Jerry. I suppose they would have enjoyed the game even if Jerry didn't play, just for the experience of being there, but that wasn't the point.

He didn't play the third quarter either and the Warriors fell behind by six. When the Bucks started off the fourth quarter with six straight points to lead by twelve, *then* they put in Jerry and the magic started all over again. Maybe it was because he knew we were there or maybe it's just because he really is the greatest, I don't know. Bert had sent him a telegram saying we were gonna be there, so I like to think it was us inspiring him.

Jerry brought the ball downcourt and drilled one in from twenty-five feet. Then Alvin blocked a shot, grabbed the ball and hit Jerry with an outlet pass and Jerry went all the way the length of the court and scored on a spectacular layup *and* he was fouled. He sank the free throw and then stole the inbound pass and scored again! Seven straight points he'd scored and everybody in the pavilion was on their feet screaming. The Bucks looked just as bewildered as Portland had. But pretty soon they were more than bewildered they were calling time out. Jerry was just killing them. The Warriors just kept feeding Jerry and he kept scoring from everywhere. Finally the Bucks started double-teaming him and he just passed off to the open man and there was nothing they could do about it. He finished the game with twenty-one points and the Warriors won by seven. When the game ended, pandemonium broke out. It was like they'd won a championship or something.

We waited around for forty-five minutes but Jerry couldn't have gotten out to us if he'd wanted to, the crowd of people hanging around was so huge.

35

The next day the sports page headlines in the *Chronicle* were SUPER SUB STUNS BUCKS. The sports columnist gave Jerry half a column.

The Golden State Warriors unleashed their secret weapon in the 4th quarter of last night's contest with the powerful Milwaukee Bucks and it proved to be more than the boys from Schlitz town could handle. Jerry Maxwell turned in his second clutch performance in as many games, to lead the otherwise weary Warriors to their second straight come-from-behind victory. Maxwell scored an amazing twenty-one points in a little less than twelve minutes. He had three assists, four steals and one very timely offensive rebound that he turned into a three-point play. His shooting percentage was phenomenal. 100% from the free-throw line, eight of nine from the field. Mr. Maxwell, who isn't going to stay much of a secret for very long, is also the shortest man in the NBA at 5'9". Reports are that Maxwell is still recuperating from surgery he underwent less than a year ago. When he recovers fully, I pity the man or men given the assignment of trying to stop him.

About noontime that day, I got a call from Jerry. Before I could congratulate him on his game he invited me, Jackson, Bert and Louise to a party at Alvin's that night.

"What kind of party is it?" I asked.

"Well, we're leaving for a road trip tomorrow and so Ellen thought it would be nice to have a few people over for dinner," he says. "You think you'll all be able to make it?"

"How many people is a few?" I ask.

"Maybe twenty," he says.

"Aw Jerry," I said, "I'd feel out of place."

"It'll be nice," he said. "You'll know half of them. You, Bert, Jackson, Louise, Al, Ellen and me. The rest are just friends of Al's and Ellen's. I don't know 'em either. What do you say?"

"Okay," I said, "but I don't have any fancy clothes."

"Don't worry about it," he says.

Good old Bert called Jerry right back and asked if he could bring Edith along. Jerry said sure, he had meant to invite her too. It had just slipped his mind, he said.

So we all drove down in Jackson's car and I tried not to but I ended up describing Alvin's house the whole way down. We were all dressed pretty fancy. I'd gone out and bought a new shirt and had my hair trimmed a little. I'd actually lost about ten pounds by then but I'm sure I gained five back on the hors d'oeuvres before dinner.

Joseph and his wife Miyoshi were there too, so really there were only about ten totally new faces for me to cope with. We had a great time. First we toured the house and grounds, the garden was lighted beautifully, and then we went into the huge living room for drinks and socializing before dinner.

Jerry and Louise got together again and there was no getting them apart all evening practically. At one point they disappeared for about a half hour and later on I found out they'd gone walking out by the pool.

Edith teased Jerry about not inviting her, but Jerry got out of that by saying he knew Bert was sweet on her and going to ask her anyway. Jackson had Alvin and Ellen and two other black couples just dying the whole time, which proves he's not just funny at Max's.

Then we had an incredible seafood dinner with wine, and for dessert we had flaming ice cream cake. I would have felt terrible making such a pig of myself, but with all the athletes putting it away I didn't have to worry about that.

Then we just sat around talking and Jerry came up to me and said he wanted to talk to me alone. So we went outside into the inner garden and sat down on the bench by the pond and he said, "So how you doin, Roary? You enjoying the party?"

"I love it," I said, "it's like a dream. This whole damn week seems like a dream."

"I know," he said, shaking his head and grinning at me. "Roary, I think I'm gonna be buying a house around here. They're already saying if I pan out they'll pay me a lot of money to play for them next year and so I thought it would be nice to live near Alvin, but I also want to live near you. So I was wondering, if I got a place with a guest house, if maybe you'd like to live there."

That made me feel very strange. I had always wanted to live near Jerry in some nice place, but everything was different now. I could just see myself being the weird old cripple who lived in the famous Jerry Maxwell's guest house. It seemed like a stupid idea. "No," I said, "that really sounds nice, Jerry, but my home is Max's, you know? But get the guest house anyway so I can visit you without having to stay at the Busy Bee Motel this time."

He smiled a little and said, "That was the old Jerry. That was really rotten of me, Roary, and I'm sorry. I'm done with caring what other people think. I'm just gonna do what I want from now on."

"Like what?" I asked.

"Like have a good time," he said, giving me a wicked little smile that didn't seem like him at all.

"Good for you, Jerry," I said. "It's about time."

Then we went inside and I couldn't wait to leave, to sit in the car with the gang and hear them discuss their impressions of the party, the house, everything. But before we left, Alvin gave each of us a glass and poured us each a little wine and said, "Here's to the ultimate victory, whatever it is for each of us." We drank the wine and then Jackson said, "Yeah, and here's to you guys winning the playoffs, as mundane as that may be."

On the way home Louise couldn't stop talking about the house, the gorgeous clothes people were wearing, Jerry, what a sweetheart he was. Edith couldn't stop talking about the food. Christ, we relived every course of dinner in detail and I got hungry all over again. Bert talked about the quality wines and the swimming pool, and Jackson for once didn't say much of anything.

36

The next week was unbelievable. Every day there was stuff in the paper about Jerry. He was playing more and more, constantly surprising people. The Warriors won three out of their four games on the road and Jerry was averaging thirteen points a game even though he was only playing about half of each game. A kind of ironic thing happened too, they nicknamed him Super Max because his last name was Maxwell. Some player on the New York Knicks called him that and it stuck. I kept thinking, If they only knew he was Super Max from Max's. Jackson started teasing Max about really being Jerry's long-lost father. Max would smile a little, sip his beer and say nothing, as if to say, "Believe anything you like, that's what I'm here for."

Then Bert stunned us with the news that he had leased the building next door and had gotten permission to knock out the walls and connect the two buildings so we could expand

Max's, build a stage, get some pool tables and maybe put in a delicatessen section.

Then Jackson announced he was getting married to a woman named Flora Johnson. I went around for a day refusing to believe him, but he was not only really getting married, he was getting married right away. It felt a little weird to have Jackson marrying somebody I didn't even know. It made me realize how little I really knew about him, how little of his private life he brought to Max's. Bert was the only person I knew who'd ever even met Flora.

So anyway, two days later Jackson got married to her in a private ceremony at Flora's parents' house. Only their families were there but the next day we had an after-lunch reception at Max's so we could all meet the bride. We all got to kiss Flora hello and, as Jackson put it, "get a look at the merchandise." The merchandise is the type of person who would never seriously allow anybody to call her merchandise, being that she's a very strong, liberated kind of woman, but she was letting Jackson fool around in front of his friends.

She wasn't at all what I'd expected. I imagined Jackson would marry somebody who looked like Alvin's wife, you know, real tall and graceful. Flora is short, incredibly energetic and beautiful, but not in the classic way Ellen is. There's a lot of fierceness in her face. She's very dark, her hair is very short like they wear it in Africa, and her eyes are enormous. She has very round cheeks too. The main thing about her is that she's really intense. When she listens to you, you feel like she's devouring your words. She teaches sociology at San Francisco State.

So Jackson passed out cigars to everybody and then he said, "And now, my friends, Ms. Johnson and I have a plane to catch." He got a great snooty look on his face and suddenly had a British accent. "We're off to Kenya, you see, for a week or so. Big-game hunting and all that rot. Lions and tigers and zebras and hippopotomi and elephant of course. I'll bring you all a tusk." Actually they were going to Acapulco for two weeks, which meant we all had to take on another two hours of work a day until he came back.

As if all that wasn't enough for one week, Louise goes and gets a big part in a play, nothing big time, but a lead just the same, and she goes directly to heaven and stays there for a few days.

So on Saturday night I take Louise out to dinner and to the ballet to celebrate. Who knows why, but afterwards at her place that night, I kissed her, she allowed it, and then when I got a little more passionate she started to cry.

"Oh, Roary," she said, hugging me, "I think you're a really nice guy but . . ."

So I left. I knew I was being stupid to try and love her that way. I really don't know why I did it except I guess all the excitement, all the good feelings from Jackson's marriage, Jerry's success, Max's changing, I guess I felt like all that was going to change me too. But it wouldn't have been so bad really, just a little misunderstanding, because I wasn't really hurt by it, I understood, but I guess Louise didn't, because the next day she called up Bert and told him she was quitting her job at Max's.

I went over to her place that afternoon.

Louise lives in the bottom half of an old Victorian house over in the gay part of San Francisco, near Castro Street. She's got a cat, lots of plants, some really nice old antique furniture. You feel like you're in a play just being there.

I knock on her door. "Who is it?" she asks, like she was afraid of something.

"Me," I said.

"Please go away, Roary," she said, doing her determined-woman bit. Part of Louise's problem is that she's seen too many old movies. Sometimes she gets carried away.

"No, Louise," I say. "We have to talk."

"There's nothing to say," she says, sounding like Bette Davis.

"Bullshit, Louise," I say. I wasn't nervous. It really hadn't meant that much to me. Louise did, but the whole physical attempt had been more a symbolic act, I think, than a real attempt at lovemaking, at least that's the way I was looking at it.

"Please go away," she said, not so determined any more.

"I just want five minutes," I told her.

She finally let me in. She was wearing an old Chinese silk bathrobe and she'd been crying, so her makeup had run all over her face. She looked awful. I got right to the point. "Look," I said, "It's not like some Gothic romance. I'm not going to mope around wounded for the rest of my life. I love you as a friend, Louise. I got carried away. So we won't be lovers, big deal."

"I've hurt you, Roary," she says, looking away dramatically. She's really a good actress, in my opinion.

"Quit projecting," I said, only this time I meant it. "Look, when I kissed you, it was because I was happy about the ballet, about Jerry, about everything. The rest of it was stupid. It doesn't mean I lie awake horny for you, Louise. I don't. So why are you quitting Max's? We need you, the guys need you, and you need the job, and besides you're my friend."

"Roary," she says, "I know why you're saying this. It doesn't change a thing. It doesn't change what I know."

"Which is?"

"Which is that you are a desperately lonely man and I rejected you for no good reason."

I thought about that. Lonely man. That was true some of the time. But rejected for no good reason? "Look," I said, "lots of people I like as friends I wouldn't want to go to bed with. I don't have to leave the country because of it."

"Roary," she said, turning on me suddenly, "I love you."

"Good," I said, "I love you too. Let's be friends, okay, and forget that other crap."

"You don't understand," she said, raising her voice, "I *want* to love you, as a lover."

This confused me. What is she talking about?

"I'd like nothing better than to be your lover, Roary," she

says. "But I've never been able to love . . . another cripple, that way. I know it's all in my head and that it doesn't make sense, but I still can't. And knowing that I love you and can't love you . . . that's the reason I'm quitting."

"Look," I said, sort of stunned by the whole thing, "it was my fault for trying to kiss you."

"No," she said, shaking her head, "I would have quit soon anyway."

"But not because of me," I said. "I'm too fat and hairy, remember?" I was trying to make a joke.

"Oh, who gives a shit about that!" she screams. "Why do you think I fed you all that crap about losing weight? That was as much *my* excuse as yours!"

"Okay," I said, sitting down. My mind was overloaded. Things seemed so complicated all of a sudden. "How about this? How about if you stay on until we find somebody new? I won't work there when you're there. How about that?"

That just made it worse. She really started crying then.

"How about this?" I said, when she finally stopped crying. "How about if we try to work it out, slowly, and you stay at Max's and see how it goes?"

37

So suddenly I'm in love, or maybe I was in love all along but I hadn't let myself think it. Louise and I started spending a couple evenings a week together after she'd get done with her play rehearsal. Nothing very sexual or anything happened but we held hands a lot, did some kissing, and I started to feel so good I stopped eating in between meals. My clothes started getting too big for me. I actually got a pretty short haircut, short for me anyway, and Louise trimmed my beard.

The best part, though, was the talking. I realized that in all the time I'd known Jerry we had never really talked about deep things. We didn't try to work on our problems together. Mainly we just accepted each other, which was incredibly important to me, but with Louise there was that and then a deeper knowledge of each other too. The thing that bonded me to Jerry was that he trusted me with his secrets, which made me feel special, which was what I had needed to feel.

So all this great stuff is going on at Max's and Louise's play is going along just fine and the Warriors come home from their road trip to finish off the regular season in Oakland. And then the most incredible thing happens. *Sports Illustrated* arrives and you'll never guess who's on the front cover. Sure it's a picture of three Warriors and two Knicks players too, but there's Jerry right in the middle of them, hanging in midair, the ball in his hands, his muscles bulging as he flies towards the basket. The caption reads WARRIOR SPARKPLUG JERRY MAXWELL.

I sat there in Max's looking at the picture for at least ten minutes. I'd already looked at it for half an hour at home and I was gonna show it to Bert, but when I got to Max's I had to sit down and look at it again there. It's four o'clock, things are pretty slow. I look around the joint. There's some guys crowded around the pinball machine, Stinky is playing gin rummy with Max at the bar. Bert's taking inventory. It's the lull before the storm. After five the place is gonna be jammed. All those guys getting off work, getting out of bed, coming in for their fix of booze and companionship. And here's Jerry putting the moves on some poor bastard in Madison Square Garden. Here's Jerry dressed in a golden jersey, number eight, playing with guys he used to worship. Max's I can handle. Louise in a play, it's a little much but I can deal with it. But not this other thing. Not Jerry on the cover of *Sports Illustrated*.

I drop the magazine on the bar for Bert to look at and then I walk out. I'm out the door and down the street a ways before I hear him shout. I can just picture in my mind all those guys stampeding to the bar to take a look.

I wander down towards the park. It looks like rain but not for a while. I stop in front of a little joint that sells Greek food, the baklava looks good but I pass. There's the usual garbage in the gutters, dog crap on the sidewalk, beautiful teeny three-year-old Chinese kids crossing the street by themselves in heavy traffic, a crazy guy with long matted brown hair and greasy mechanic's overalls standing on the corner screaming about Fascists and Jesus. There's people double-parked all over the place. Two Spanish ladies, each weighing about three hundred pounds walk towards me. They've both got baskets full of flowers. They're chattering away in Spanish, a thousand words a minute, and they hardly see me as they go by. It's a regular day. And it seems like this is reality. And *Sports Illustrated* isn't reality. It's fairy tales to help you sleep at night.

I cut over to Edison and sit down on a bench to watch the black boys playing ball. One guy waves to me. He used to play with Jerry. Or Jerry used to play with him. And I realize that these guys probably don't know about Jerry any more. In fact, I'm sure of it. If you told them Jerry was a pro now, they'd laugh. They'd say, "Jerry? The gimp? Come on, man, the guy could shoot, but cripples don't make it in the pros." Playgrounds don't turn into Madison Square Garden. Whores don't turn into virgin pompom girls, except in our dreams.

Anyway, after about three weeks of rehearsal, which Louise said wasn't enough, her play opens. I'm there early on opening night, best seat in the house, if you can call it a house. It's one of those tiny theaters that seats maybe a hundred people and was probably once a striptease joint or just a bar. It's in North Beach in the middle of all the topless joints and it's pretty strange going past all the flashy whores and transvestites and wide-eyed tourists to get there, but it's nice inside, very intimate and I'm thrilled to death because pretty soon Louise is gonna be acting right there in front of me.

It's a play about two women who are in love with a third woman. I read it before I saw it and I just couldn't imagine Louise playing the part she had. The part was of this crazy, fairly violent woman, the woman the two women love. The name of the play was *Periwinkles*, which I looked up in the dictionary. It's either a sea snail or a solitary flower. I think in this case it means solitary flowers.

So I'm sitting there about ten minutes before it starts and Jerry and Alvin and Ellen show up. Jerry's real glad to see me and so are Alvin and Ellen for some reason. They're all dressed to the teeth and Jerry looks better than ever. But what's weird is, I'm not glad to see them. I wanted to just concentrate on Louise that night. But in another way I'm glad they're there because Louise will be thrilled.

The play is good, I think, but very depressing. What saves it is Louise. She is just fabulous. She becomes this other woman completely. She's so full of violence and hatred it's scary, but it's not phony at all. I believe she is this other woman.

As it turned out, Louise got pretty good reviews even though the show got bad reviews and closed after a few weeks. But that first-night audience went nuts applauding at the end. And they brought flowers out to Louise, which seemed really wonderful to me until I found out Jerry had sent them. I found out backstage when Louise came rushing out of her dressing room, hugged me and said, "Where's Jerry? Oh God, he sent me flowers!"

Now, the reason I didn't send her flowers was because I wanted to see if the play was any good or not first. What if she'd been lousy? What if the audience had booed? Flowers? It would have been ridiculous.

We all went out afterwards to the bar on top of the Fairmount Hotel. We drove over in Alvin's Mercedes. Louise was just ecstatic. I was enjoying it, mainly because she kept hugging me, but I started feeling pretty weird because she was hugging Jerry too.

We had champagne, caviar, the works. There was a good dance band playing and Louise danced the first dance with me, a slow one, but afterwards she danced with Jerry pretty much and a couple times with Alvin. I stayed at the table and talked to Ellen. She said she'd been waiting for a chance to get to know me better, which struck me as about the nicest thing anybody could ever say to me. I got pretty drunk, told her a bunch of stupid stories about myself and then I told her she looked Egyptian to me, like an Egyptian queen. She blushed, then smiled and said, "For that you get a dance." So we got up and she held me close and we danced real slow for a long time and I let myself have this wild fantasy where Ellen can't help herself and she falls madly in love with me and we run off together to Europe, and we actually make love on the jet on the way over.

38

The next day at Max's, Louise comes in with the reviews of her play. She's pissed off that the play got bad reviews but she's ecstatic about her good reviews. One guy said her performance was "dazzling." She's wearing a very fancy black antique dress, her hair is all curled and she's got on more makeup than usual.

"You look great," I say, hugging her. "What's the occasion?"

"Oh God," she says, rolling her eyes, "Jerry's taking me to lunch. And tonight I'm going to the game with Ellen. Isn't that wonderful?" She smiles at me like I'm her dear sweet old father or something, like I'm supposed to pat her on the head and say good girl or something.

"Swell," I say, without much feeling.

"Are you going to the game?" she asks, casually.

"No," I say, though I had tickets.

"There's only three more regular season games," she said seriously. "You oughta go."

"Christ," I yell, "you didn't know a regular season game from a doughnut two weeks ago!"

"Good grief, Roary," she says, grimacing at me, "don't be such a child." And then she turns around and walks out.

Needless to say, I'm incensed. I'm also sort of nauseated because my system isn't geared for hating the people I love, though that's what I was trying to do. I wished Jackson was back from Acapulco so I could explode at someone, get all my feelings out, but there's only Bert and he always thinks I'm overreacting. So I'm standing there behind the bar about to explode when Max calls to me.

"Hey Roary," he says.

I go over to him. I think the earthquake could hit and if Max wanted to talk to me I'd go over and listen to him. To me, Max is the most fascinating person in the world, probably because I don't know the first thing about him after knowing him for almost three years. "Yeah, Max?" I say.

"What's the problem?" he asks, sipping his beer.

I can't believe he asked me. I'm stunned. I stand there speechless and forget what I'm mad about.

"If it's Louise," he says, cocking his head to one side and smiling just the tiniest bit, "just remember she loves you. Whatever happens, there's always that."

"It's more complicated than that," I say, feeling almost hypnotized by him.

"No," he says very quietly. "On the surface it's complicated. Underneath, she loves you."

"Yeah, but that doesn't mean she won't go fall in love with Jerry," I say, feeling my anger coming back.

"You never have anything but that," he says reaching out his hand and touching my forehead with his tiny index finger.

"Okay," I said, blinking. "Thanks."

Max nods. That's it. He's done talking. He sips his beer and doesn't say another word.

But even with Max's little pep talk, despite the truth of it, I feel so hurt by Louise and Jerry that I decide I never want to see either of them again. I'm not being real rational but that's what I decide. So I don't go to the game that night and I take the next day off and stay home making myself madder and madder.

I get the morning paper and see that Jerry scored twenty points, but the Warriors lost. I couldn't be more pleased. But then in my jealous frame of mind I have Louise consoling Jerry afterwards and they end up going to bed together and I get even madder.

So when I know Louise is done at Max's, I go down and get into a card game with Stinky, Blue and Wings. My plan is to get drunk and eat a lot of junk. Stinky is cheating, as usual whenever he deals, because the cards have braille bumps and things are going along pretty normally when Wings says, "I guess Louise has really gone and flipped over Jerry."

"Yeah?" says Stinky. "Really? You think they'll get married?"

"Probably not," says Blue, shaking his head. "Jerry can have his pick now that he's a star."

"What does that mean?" I ask, glowering at him.

"Aw shit, I don't know," he says. "Just came out. I'm just talking."

"They're going out tonight, aren't they?" asks Stinky.

"Tomorrow night, I thought," says Wings.

"Excuse me," I say, getting up to go. "I'm out."

If Louise was going out with Jerry the next night it meant she'd forgotten I was supposed to come over for dinner after her play. This was too much for me.

I went home and called Louise, and then I remembered she was in her play. So then I called Jerry at Alvin's. I knew they weren't playing that night and I thought maybe he'd be home. He was.

"Hey Roary," he said, sounding cheerful, "I was just thinking about you."

"Yeah?" I said, "you got a nice doghouse for me to sleep in, Jerry. You know, out in back of the guest house?"

"What?" he said, shocked.

"You got a doghouse for me?" I say. "You want me to pimp for you, Jerry?"

"Is this a joke?" he asks. "Are you all right?"

"Yeah, I'm all right, Jerry. You're the one who's not all right. You know what you are? You're a fucking rat. A goddamn backstabbing, insensitive, thankless shithead and I've had it, had it up over my head, so I'm choking on all the shit you've dumped on me. Well I don't want any more of it, see. No more. Ever. I don't ever want to see you or hear you again!"

"Roary . . ." he says, but I hang up.

The next night, Thursday, I was supposed to go over to Louise's for a midnight dinner after her play. But I figured she was going out with Jerry and besides, I told myself, I hated her now so I didn't have to even think about it. I knew Jerry had a game that night and I could just see him in the locker room afterwards, Alvin saying, "Where you going, Jer?" and Jerry saying, "Oh, I got a hot date with Louise." And Alvin saying, "Hey hey, Jer. Get it on!" Which I know Alvin would never say, but that's the scene I ran in my mind.

I'd skipped work for a second day mainly because my back was killing me. I was gonna go to the movies that night, but I figured I'd stay home and watch TV instead, get drunk and eat lots of cookies and crap. I'd been on a two-day binge and I felt horrible. Then at twelve-fifteen that night Louise calls me.

"What happened?" she says, sounding a little worried. "I thought you were coming to the play."

"Oh, really?" I say.

There's a long pause, then she says, "Are you coming over for dinner?"

"What for?" I ask, monotone.

"Hey," she says, trying to be cheerful, "just come over, okay?"

"Why?" I say, still monotone.

"For dinner. To eat," she says. "Are you all right?"

"Am I?" I say.

"I don't know," she says, laughing. "Come over and I'll take a look."

"Very funny," I say with as little feeling as possible.

"I'm even funnier in person," she says. "Just come over, okay?"

I wasn't going to go. I was trying to get her upset so she'd tell me to go to hell, but it was like she knew what I was trying to do, and no matter how obnoxious I got she just kept asking me to come over.

So I went, half expecting Jerry to be there. When I got to her house I peeked in the window and I could see her setting the table for two, which meant Jerry wasn't there, so I figured she was planning to butter me up before she told me she was in love with him.

When she answered the door she gave me a big hug, even though I was scowling, and then she said, "I hope you're hungry because there's tons."

I walk in without saying anything and plop down on the couch. Louise heads for the kitchen. "Dinner's ready," she says.

I stay on the couch. I'm feeling so many things I can't move. I can feel this incredible confrontation coming and I can't move. She comes back from the kitchen with two plates of food. "Come eat," she says, setting the food down on the table and coming over to me. She's got her hair tied back in a ponytail and almost no makeup on. She's wearing a long patchwork skirt and a white Mexican blouse. She looks

141

terrific as usual. She reaches out her hands to me. I'm supposed to take them and then she'll pull me up and we'll go to the table. But I don't take her hands. I just sit there.

She hesitates for a moment, then sits down beside me and takes my hand. I don't think she would have done that if she'd known what kind of hatred was in me right then. I expected her to say something like, "What's wrong?" but she doesn't say anything. She just sits there holding my hand. Then she leans her head on my shoulder, sighs and closes her eyes.

We sat there for a long time. The food stopped steaming and the traffic noise died down, which meant it was really late. My anger would well up and I'd feel like pushing her away and screaming at her, and then it would subside and I'd feel very sad. And sometimes I'd feel love for her. I'd feel like putting my arms around her and kissing her. But instead we just sat, each of us waiting for the other person to speak.

Finally I mumbled, "I better go."

"I love you," she says, very quietly.

I don't say anything. I feel my anger coming back and I tense up.

She holds my hand tighter, keeps her head on my shoulder and says, "I love you, Roary. I don't love Jerry." She sniffles and I realize she's been crying silently. I look down at her and I see her cheeks are wet. "I think he's sweet, you know?" she says. "I was flattered. It was nice to get flowers, to go to a fancy restaurant. There's nothing wrong with that, is there?"

"No," I said.

"But when he said he wanted to see me all the time, I told him that I was, you know, with you."

"You said that to him?" I said, amazed. She nodded. "You said you were with *me*?" I ask again.

"I told him we were lovers," she said, pulling away from me a little and smiling at me.

"God, I wish you'd told me all this last week," I said.

"I didn't know last week," she said, shrugging her shoulders.

142

I laughed. I couldn't help it.

"What's so funny?" she asks.

"I don't know," I say, shaking my head.

She puts her arms around me and kisses me. "You really love me?" I ask, still not believing this is happening.

She doesn't say anything. She just kisses me again, and then the most incredible thing happened. I wasn't even thinking about it, but we just got going and the next thing I knew we were in bed making love.

39

During breakfast the next morning, Louise told me that when she told Jerry she was in love with me, he was totally shocked. She said he got very agitated and then really worried. He said he hadn't known that Louise and I were involved romantically, that I never told him. This was all before my crazy phone call. He told her that when he'd asked me about her, I had said that she was unattached and available, which of course was true, which made me feel so bad about what I'd said on the phone to him, I couldn't think of anything but getting hold of Jerry and begging him to forgive me.

So I'm hurrying to catch the bus, shuffling fast along Castro Street, when whammo here's Ann. She doesn't recognize me. She's leaning against a wall, staring down at the ground. Her hair is all ratty and her little red skirt that barely covers her ass looks pretty silly so early in the morning. So does her black lace blouse and the ugly gray sweater she must have picked up at the Salvation Army. And what's she doing on Castro Street, I wonder. I figure she must be hustling dykes.

She looks about the same from a distance, but when I get closer to her I realize she's gotten real skinny and her face has really changed. She's not even shot beautiful any more. She's just shot. Seeing her there just kills me. Part of me wants to just go by and forget about her, but another part says I have to stop, so I do.

"Ann?" I say, coming up to her.

She looks up at me slowly. She doesn't recognize me.

"Ann?" I say again. "It's me, Roary. From Max's. Remember? I'm a friend of Jerry's."

"Jerry?" she says, looking around. "Where's Jerry?"

"He's not here," I say. "Do you remember me?"

"Of course I remember you," she says. "Roary. A friend of Jerry's." She smiles a phony smile at me.

"You hungry?" I ask. I don't know why I said that, except that she looks like she's starving to death.

"I'll give you a blow job for five bucks," she says, the smile still on her face.

"I don't want a blow job," I say. "Let me buy you some breakfast."

She stares at me for a moment and then she really does recognize me. "Roary," she says, a little life in her voice. "You lost weight. Shit, I didn't recognize you. Shit, you look great."

"Thanks," I say. "How about breakfast?"

"Breakfast sure," she says.

So we go into the first little cafe we come to and, Christ, you should have seen Ann put the food away. She ordered some eggs and waffles, finished those in a minute and then, when I said she should have something else, she had a big omelet and then a milkshake. Then she drank about five cups of coffee and had three doughnuts.

"Hungry, huh?" I said.

She pushed her hair out of her face, sat up straight and looked me right in the eye. "You want something?" she asks.

"Me? No," I say. "I wanted to buy you breakfast, that's all."

"Are you gay?" she asked, which is a reasonable question considering where I ran into her.

"No," I said.

144

"So maybe I can do something for you," she says, very matter-of-factly.

"I have a girlfriend," I say, feeling uncomfortable.

"Shit, Roary," she says, laughing this deep strange laugh, "I know some tricks you would *not* believe. Not believe."

"I just wanted to buy you some breakfast," I say, fidgeting.

"You ever gotten off three times in less than an hour?" she asks, arching her eyebrows. "I know a way. It'll blow your mind."

"Look, Ann," I say, looking around the room thinking of a hundred things I want to say to her, "I don't *want* anything."

She smiles at me and sucks real hard on her cigarette. "You just saw me on the corner, you were overwhelmed with compassion, and for old times' sake you thought you'd buy me some breakfast."

"Something like that," I say.

"I may puke," she says.

I can't think of how to say any of the things I want to say. I just sit there looking at her. I'm thinking about Jerry when they used to live together and it seems like fifty years ago. I feel like an old man looking back through time.

"I'm sorry," she says. "You always were a sap. Thanks for breakfast."

"You're welcome," I say.

She gets up and goes to the ladies room. I leave the tip, pay the bill and then I go outside and wait for her. She comes out a minute later and says, "You got fifty dollars I can borrow?"

"No," I say.

"Come on," she says, "be a sap. It's fucking cold in the morning. I need a coat."

"Ask your pimp for a coat," I say.

She laughs at that and shakes her head. "You be my pimp," she says. "How about twenty-five, Roary?"

"For junk?" I ask, "or for a coat?"

"Come on, Roary," she says. "For old times' sake."

Who knows why but I give her twenty-five, and as I'm giving it to her I mumble something like, "Aren't you even gonna ask about Jerry?"

She takes the money and laughs at me. "You think I don't know about Jerry?" she says, shaking her head and giving me this sneery smile.

"I don't know," I said. "Do you?"

"Of course I do!" she screams. "That little prick is gonna limp around that fuckin freak house for the rest of his life! Because he's nothing!" She's trembling now and I think maybe she's gonna cry but she doesn't. Then she calms down. "And you're a sap," she says. "And I'm a whore. And that's the way it is."

"Maybe so," I say.

"Thanks again for breakfast," she says, heading back to her corner. Then she stops, looks at the money in her hands and laughs that deep vicious laugh. "You coulda got a lot for this," she says.

"Happy birthday," I say.

"Fuck you," she says, smiling sweetly.

40

I pick up a morning paper before I get back to my apartment after running into Ann. I flip back to the sports page to see how Jerry's doing. The Warriors won a close one but apparently Jerry didn't play. He's not listed in the box score. I get home, sit down and read the article on the game. There's not a word about Jerry. It's like he's suddenly disappeared.

So I call Alvin's, but nobody's home. It's about ten-thirty so I shower up, change my clothes and head down to Max's. I open up and go in. Max is already by the cash register, reading the morning paper.

"Hey Max," I say. He doesn't say anything, which is perfectly normal, but I feel like talking, so I say, "You were right about Louise." He still doesn't say anything, so I shut up and get the floor swept before the regulars start wandering in.

I'm still thinking about Ann, trying to decide whether to tell Jerry about her or not, when Alvin Martin comes striding into Max's, and I mean striding. He's wearing old jeans and a sweatshirt. He's not his usual stylish self. "Hey Alvin," I say.

He has this fierce look on his face. He obviously hasn't had much sleep lately. "Where's Jerry?" he asks.

"Jerry?" I say. "I don't know. With you, I thought."

"No," said Alvin. "He didn't show for the game last night and I've called the police, hospitals, everywhere, nothing."

"Jesus," I say, stunned.

Alvin puts his hands on the bar and bows his head. "You know him better than I do. Where would he go?"

"Here, I guess, but he isn't here," I said.

"It doesn't make any sense," says Alvin. "He seemed so goddamn happy."

"He didn't say anything?" I ask, starting to feel a tingling at the back of my neck.

"Last I saw him he was going apartment hunting," says Alvin. "Seemed a little anxious but nothing unusual. Goddamn!" he says, glaring at me, "we gotta find that bastard. The playoffs start next week and I don't really care if he plays or not, but the team is completely freaked out, not to mention the coach and the general manager. The owners don't know yet, thank God. Where would that guy *go*?"

"Here," I said, "but he isn't here."

"Well, if he shows up, you clamp onto that dude and call me. All right?"

"Right," I said.

Alvin put his hand on my shoulder and broke into a big worried sort of smile. "Interesting switcheroo, huh?"

"I guess," I said, wracking my brains trying to figure out where Jerry might be.

"Call me tonight whatever," he says on his way out. "I gotta go appease the front office."

"Right," I said.

I turn and look at Max. He's sipping his beer and reading the paper. I know he's not in a talking mood but I've got to talk to him. I'm starting to realize that my calling Jerry and yelling at him and saying the things I said might have caused all this, but I'm not quite admitting it yet. "Max," I say, "where would Jerry go?"

Max looks up at me slowly, swallows and says, "Here, but he isn't here."

So the Warriors lose the last game of the season, though they still finish in first place by one game. A sports columnist in the *Chronicle* has for his headline WHERE IS JERRY MAXWELL? and goes on to analyze the Warriors, pointing up how crucial Jerry is to their playoff chances.

The official Warrior line is that Jerry had to leave town unexpectedly to clear up some personal matters and that he's expected back by the time the playoffs begin. Meanwhile Alvin calls me every morning and every evening and says, "Well?" And I say, "No luck," and my whole life seems suspended while we wait for Jerry.

Then two days before the playoffs start, this is five days after Jerry disappeared, Jackson comes back from Acapulco. That cheers everybody else up, but like I said, my whole life is in limbo until Jerry comes back. Then the next day the work starts on Max's. Bert hired a crew of really hip long-haired guys and arranged for as many guys at Max's who want to, to work with them. It really is an exciting time for most of the guys, but not for me. I get myself so agitated that the day the playoffs are going to start, I can't go to work.

It's around lunchtime and I'm lying on my waterbed watching a soap opera, keeping myself numb with beer, when the phone rings. It's Jerry. I practically faint when I hear his voice. "Hello, Roary," he says. He sounds very far away.

"Jerry," I say. "Where are you?"

"I'm . . . uh . . . I wanted to talk to you. Can I come over?" He sounds very unsure of himself, almost like he's afraid of me.

"Sure," I say. "Sure, yeah, come over. Where are you?"

"Listen," he says, ignoring my question, "don't call Alvin or anybody, okay?"

"Okay," I said.

"I'll be over in an hour or so," he says.

"Okay," I say. "Hurry it up."

I'm tempted to call Alvin but I don't. Instead I go out and get some more beer and pretzels. I'm very excited. I'm rehearsing what I'm going to say to him all the way to the store and back.

He doesn't come for almost two hours and I practically go crazy that last half hour. But finally he arrives. I open the door and there he is, but he doesn't look so terrific any more. In fact, he looks like he hasn't eaten or shaved in about a week. It turns out he hasn't.

"Jesus, Jerry," I say, "where've you been?"

He walks past me, sits down on the couch and then he covers his eyes.

I don't know what to do. I feel completely responsible for him but I don't know what to do. I sit down beside him, but I don't touch him. "Hey," I say. "I was wrong. I'm sorry."

He looks up at me wild-eyed. "No you weren't wrong, Roary," he says very excitedly. "You were right. Everything you said was right."

"Aw come on, Jerry, you didn't know I was in love with Louise. I didn't tell you."

"Of course I knew," he says. "You think I'm dumb? You think I couldn't see you were in love with her?"

"Well, even so, you didn't know she . . ."

"Oh for Chrissake, Roary!" he says angrily, "I used you. I used you every chance I got. From the very beginning. And when I was done using you, I forgot about you. I didn't call you for four months!"

"You were busy," I said.

149

"No!" he shouts. "I just didn't have any use for you."

"You didn't?" I say, starting to feel a tightness in my throat.

"I pretended to love people," he says sadly. "I pretended to love Ann, to love the guys. All I ever really cared about was me."

"Not true," I said.

"Whatdaya mean, not true?" he says, glaring at me. "I've been riding around on a Greyhound bus for five days straight. Not eating or sleeping or talking, just thinking. And I come up with nothing."

"Big deal Jerry, so it took you a little longer to get your miracle," I say.

"What?" he shouts. "What the fuck are you talking about?"

"To get your leg right."

"Forget about my leg!" he screams. "I am not my leg!"

"Okay Jerry," I say, "I'll forget about your leg. You're still my friend."

"Why?" he asks. "Why?" he says again, raising his hands in the air and then dropping them.

"Because you made me feel alive when I felt like dying," I say.

"Oh bullshit," he says, looking away.

"Besides," I say, "you're not such a great actor, you know. You couldn't fake it for that long."

"Fake what?" he asks, wrinkling his brow. "What are you talking about?"

"You can't fake love for more than a few days," I say. "Come on, Jerry, think about it. Think about Stinky. You love him?"

"Well sure, Stinky, but . . ."

"Max?"

"Yeah but . . ."

"Bert, Jackson, Edith? Admit it, you fuckin love everybody."

"But . . ." he says, shaking his head.

"And I'll tell you something else. Alvin, the guy you've been pretending to love for the last two years? You better call him before he has a heart attack."

Jerry sighs and shakes his head again. "I think I'm gonna quit. I think maybe I should quit."

"And do what?" I say, shouting a little, "take up water polo?"

"I don't know," he says. "Go away, start over, try to do it right this time."

"Oh for Chrissake Jerry, just do it right here," I said, getting mad.

Then he looks at me and says very seriously, "You're such a fuckin idiot, Roary."

"I know," I said. "Every time I see you and realize you're my best friend, the depth of my idiocy overwhelms me."

"Well," says Jerry, "the idiocy of my being *your* best friend is nothing compared to the stupidity of your being *my* best friend."

"There are idiots," I say, "and then there are idiots. And then there's you, Jerry, in a class all by yourself."

"Well, you should know," he says, a smile finally starting to break through, and I can hear in his voice that he's okay, that things are gonna get rolling again.

41

So Jerry went back to the Warriors and though they threatened to drop him and generally gave him a hard time, they were apparently pretty happy and relieved to have him back. He suited up but didn't play in the first playoff game.

I went back to Max's and started acting like a human being

again and life became very cheerful for the next week or so, except something was definitely different inside of me and I had this really strong desire to get away for a while. I had this image of myself sitting among these ancient Greek ruins, getting my life figured out. For some reason, owning part of Max's just wasn't enough for me any more. I wanted to launch into some new way of living my life.

Louise's play closed and she immediately got another part, this time in a Shakespearean play and she was in seventh heaven about that because even though it was a small part, she said the exposure would be ten times greater than with *Periwinkles*. We were spending three or four nights a week together and that was wonderful in a lot of ways and pretty difficult in a lot of others because both of us were fighting against getting too dependent on each other, which caused all sorts of arguments and misunderstandings.

Jerry took awhile to get back in shape, but by the time the Warriors finished their best-of-seven series with Detroit, which they won four to two, Jerry was pretty hot again, though he still seemed to lack some of the power he'd had when he first played for the Warriors.

And then two of the guards Jerry had been filling in for returned to the team and when the semifinal series against Milwaukee began, the papers were full of articles saying that Jerry wouldn't be playing much any more, but it was nice to have him on the bench just in case. But when the Warriors lost the first two games of the series in *Oakland* against Milwaukee, without Jerry playing, the sportswriters and fans and apparently the coach too went crazy, because in the third game, which was televised, Jerry started!

Now the night that game was on, Max's was packed. And when Jerry ran out on the big five-by-five screen and smiled out at the guys in Max's, the place went bananas. "Starting at guard, five foot nine, from San Francisco, Number 8, Jerry Maxwell." It was something.

The big question was Jerry's stamina, so he played the first quarter and skipped the second quarter. He played like a demon for most of the second half, ended up with 26 points and the Warriors won 118 to 114, and that was *in* Milwaukee. When the game ended, Max's went berserk. Guys were crying, people were hugging each other, it was insane. All these people with their happiness hooked to a ball game. No wonder I wanted to go to Europe, which isn't to say I wasn't happy. I was happy. I was just starting to feel weird about a lot of things.

The Warriors ended up taking four in a row from Milwaukee with Jerry starting every game. It was incredible to watch Jerry not only playing, but controlling the ball games. Suddenly he was the undisputed team leader. All the games were close, but the Warriors suddenly had this amazing poise. They never seemed to panic. But then they had to be that way because they were going to be facing the Boston Celtics in the championship series and the Celtics had only lost one game in their last fifteen. Jerry was the key, all the sportswriters agreed. He brought order to the team, they said. The Warriors had always been a great bunch of individuals, but never a great team. The Celtics, everyone agreed, were a great team.

If you follow sports you know what happened, but I'll tell it again anyway. The series opened in Boston and Boston killed the Warriors in the first game: 140 to 103. Ran them off the court. Jerry got 5 points, Alvin got 9 points. It was a complete joke.

The second game was closer but Boston still wins: 123 to 117. Jerry had 13 points, Alvin had 27 points, but it's obvious that Boston has so many good players they can just wear down the Warriors. Plus they have this tremendous home-court advantage.

The series then moves to Oakland and the Warriors get some revenge, though barely, winning in overtime 113 to 112. Phew. Jerry had 15 points and Alvin had 44 points. He was literally the whole game and everybody knows that can't last.

153

I remember sitting at the bar in Max's the day of the fourth game. I was playing blackjack with Bert. We'd talked basketball until we were sick of it. Still, we're wondering how we can help Jerry get going. He seems so contained those first three games, probably because he's tired. Then Stinky comes walking in with Wings and says, "Hey, we decided to call Jerry and tell him we're rooting for him. We thought we could call him from here and give everybody a chance to talk to him."

Now, *that* was a great idea. So that afternoon about three, Stinky called Jerry at Alvin's and Jerry answers the phone like he was expecting our call. Stinky talked for a minute, then Bert got on, then everybody got on. Thirty people must have talked to him, including Louise and Jackson, Edith, the carpenters, even some new guys who didn't even know him. I got on and said, "So get off your ass, Jerry, and win this stupid thing."

"Okay, Roary," he said. He sounded really happy, like hearing from us was just what he needed.

Then Bert gave the phone to Max and Max says, "Jerry, this is Max." He waits for Jerry to say hello and then he says, "I want you coming back here the world champs, okay?" Then he hung up.

"What did he say?" said Bert. Everybody's standing there frozen, waiting for Max to speak.

Max took a sip of his beer and said, "No problem. Jerry says no problem."

Jackson and Bert went to the game that night but I stayed at Max's and watched the game on television. Jerry only played a little in the first half. He looked exhausted. Alvin looked worn out too and the Celtics were up by eleven at halftime. Jerry started the second half and he played really well, he scored twenty-five points, but the Warriors ended up losing by seven and Max's was like a morgue afterwards. Boston led the series three to one, which meant they only needed one more win. The Warriors needed three in a row.

I felt like packing my bags that night, cleaning out my savings account and just going. I really wanted to do that, I'm still not exactly sure why, but I had to wait for the playoffs to end. I felt like I had to be there until it was all over.

Game number five was in Boston again. This time Jerry and Alvin both got hot and they just buried Boston, despite the Boston fans booing every time the Warriors scored. Jerry had twenty-four points and Alvin had thirty-two. But the highlight of the game was when they interviewed Jerry at halftime. The first thing he said was, "Before you ask me any questions I want to say hi to the guys at Max's." That was really a great moment for us. Jackson said, "Could we have an instant replay of that please!"

The Warriors came back to Oakland for game number six and Jerry called up and told Jackson he had six really good seats for us. Jackson, Flora, Bert, Blue, Edith and Stinky went. I stayed at Max's. I was too nervous to go to the game, and besides I wanted to keep Max's open so the guys could watch the game all together.

It was pretty tense in Max's before the game started. I had about six beers and I still couldn't loosen up. I felt like I was about to explode if I had to wait any longer. Louise came in for half an hour but I was so nervous she couldn't stand it and left. The pregame bullshit went on and on forever it seemed, three morons saying the same nonsense over and over again, all of it boiling down to whoever had the most points at the end of the game would win. Finally it started, I drank down a few more beers quickly and then I glued myself to the big screen.

The game was incredibly close and very physical. It was tied at the half and I thought I was going to throw up, the tension was so great. And then, thank God, the Warriors exploded to a twenty-point lead early in the second half and ended up winning by ten points. Jerry scored twenty-six points and Alvin had an astounding forty-seven points. The series was tied three to three. The final, the one and only championship game was to be played in Boston.

42

Which is when I decided to start my European trip, by going to Boston first, seeing the game live and then flying over to Paris. I asked Louise to go with me and she wanted to but she was committed to her play. She wanted me to wait for her to get finished with the play, but she said she'd understand if I wanted to leave right then, which I did.

So I made plans to go. I sort of conspired with Ellen to get me a ticket to the game in Boston without letting Jerry or Alvin know I was planning to be there. I had to do everything in a hurry because game number seven was only three days after game number six. I already had my passport, so really all I had to do was buy my tickets. I sort of wish I'd had a little more time for saying goodbye and stuff like that, but at the same time being forced to just get off my ass and go was probably the only way I would have done it.

We had a small private going-away party at Louise's the night before I left, just the hard core of Bert, Edith, Jackson, Flora, Stinky, Blue and Wings. Max was invited but declined. They all pitched in and bought me a good suitcase and a new raincoat.

And then I flew to Boston. Goodbye San Francisco, hello Boston, just like that. I got there about two hours before the game was supposed to start. I was in a complete daze when I called Ellen at the Hilton Hotel to see if she'd gotten me a ticket, which she had. Then I took a cab over to the Hilton, Ellen met me out front and we went out for a quick dinner. Ellen was glad to have a little conspiracy going because it took her mind off the game.

I liked Boston. It felt good to be somewhere new. The people sounded different, looked different, dressed different. The air was different. Everything was different. And for some reason I wasn't that tense. Ellen was a bundle of nerves, a beautiful bundle but a bundle all the same. I wondered if when the TV cameras were scanning the crowd and they showed Ellen, like after Alvin did something great, if they'd get me in the picture and the guys in Max's would see me.

The game, of course, was sold out and when the crowd cheered or booed it was unbelievable. Ten times as loud as in Oakland. It didn't seem possible that the Warriors could win again in Boston, and it also didn't seem very fair.

And there was Jerry, warming up, looking great. I didn't want him to know I was there, not yet anyway, I wanted to save it in case he needed a kick in the ass later on. We were only thirty feet from the court. I knew he'd probably never spot me unless I called to him, but just in case, I held my program up in front of my face the whole time before the game started. I felt a little silly but it was worth it. Ellen wanted to wave to Alvin but I wouldn't let her.

So it started. Jerry, Alvin, Duke, Rollins and C.T. starting for the Warriors. It was a great first half, close all the way, though at the end of the half Boston pulled ahead by six. It was still anybody's ball game. The problem was that Alvin was doing everything and he was getting tired fast. Jerry was passing well but he wasn't shooting much. I guess he was resting. The pressure must have been incredible. I kept expecting his leg to crumble under him. I tried not to think about it but I couldn't help myself.

So finally the second half starts and the Celtics go crazy. They're scoring every time, stealing the ball, blocking shots and pretty soon they're leading by eighteen points. Alvin is being double-teamed and the Warriors seem helpless. They call a time out and without even thinking I stand up and scream, "Jerry!"

He looks up and around and I wave and he sees me. "You're an idiot!" I scream.

He starts to walk towards me with this enormous smile on

his face, but somebody grabs him and pulls him back into the huddle around the coach. People are staring at me like I'm insane, which I am, and Ellen starts patting my knee and saying, "Come on you guys, come on."

There's about five minutes left in the third quarter. Alvin is on the bench resting. Jerry gets the inbound pass, moves towards the basket and shoots the ball from thirty feet away. Bingo. Not a great tactic, but then when you're eighteen down and sinking fast, it helps.

Well, Boston didn't know what to do with Jerry after that. He's always been an incredibly accurate shooter, a great passer, a hustler, but he's never scored more than twenty-seven points. Suddenly he's shooting the ball every time he gets it, from everywhere. He's turned into this gunner. He scores thirteen points in five minutes, steals the ball twice and ends up almost singlehandedly cutting the Celtic lead to nine points by the end of the quarter.

During the short break in between quarters, he looks over at me and shakes his head, smiling in disbelief. Then he gets Alvin to look over and he breaks into this enormous smile too. Ellen waves at them and while she's waving I notice we're being shot at by a TV camera. I can't help myself and I start waving at the camera. In my mind, I hear the guys at Max's saying, "My God, that's Roary!" and the place going wild, which I found out later is exactly what happened.

The fourth quarter begins, Alvin playing again. But for the next ten minutes it was all Jerry. He was everywhere. He drove the key, he gunned from the outside, he stole the ball, he got rebounds he never should have gotten. He went completely crazy like somebody had shot him full of speed, and no matter how crazy the Celtics tried to get back, he was always just that much crazier. And he didn't miss. It was like he couldn't miss. It was one of those times like with Alvin that couldn't happen again in a million years. With three minutes left in the game it was all tied, Jerry had forty-one points and he had the ball.

He drove past his man and went up in the air at the foul line, floating towards the basket. In midair he twisted completely around so he was facing away from the hoop, and then he hooked the ball up and in. And then he got slugged in the jaw by the elbow of the Celtic's center and Jerry went down in a heap.

The Warrior coach flew off the bench along with the trainer and doctor and I collapsed in my seat, afraid to look. "Tell me what's happening," I said to Ellen, looking down at my hands.

"He's still down," she said. "I think I saw his leg move."

"His jaw's broken," I said, not looking up. "It's gotta be."

"He's getting up!" she screamed.

He was up, walking around and *limping*. I almost threw up. It was the old Jerry for a second, the big violent limp. I closed my eyes and tried to control myself. When I opened my eyes, Jerry was refusing to come out. He was just standing there shaking his head and finally his coach backed off.

Jerry had a free throw since he'd been fouled, and he made that to give the Warriors a three-point lead. The Celtics cut it to one and then Alvin and the Celtics exchanged three baskets, which still left the Warriors up by one. Then Jerry hit a jump shot from twenty-five feet out and I could see he was still limping a little, though I suppose I might have been imagining it. Then the Celtics center scored and was fouled, made the free throw and with a minute left it was all tied up.

By now I was numb. I was watching intently but I couldn't move. Jerry scored on a tremendous drive and though he was obviously fouled, there was no call. The Celtics came back and got two to tie it. Then the Warrior center, Duke, broke free on a pass from C.T. and dunked the ball to leave the Warriors up by two with thirty seconds left. Boston came down and though they missed their first shot, they scored on the rebound to tie it. Twenty seconds left. Warriors call a time out.

Days seemed to pass in those two minutes. Then the Warriors inbounded to Alvin, he shot from close in and missed! The Celtics grabbed the rebound and called time with twelve seconds left. Alvin was storming around the court claiming he'd been fouled. It took Jerry and another guy to calm him down. The whole season came down to twelve seconds. The Celtics would obviously try to run the clock down to a few seconds left and then shoot. If they scored they'd win, if they missed, overtime. In other words, they were in command.

The ball comes in to Jerry's man. Jerry's on him tight. He slips past Jerry and Jerry makes a grab for the ball, misses and *falls down!* I can't believe it. I shut my eyes, then open them and start screaming, "Get up you sonofabitch!" The roof is about to come off Boston Garden, the crowd is roaring so loud.

So Jerry's man is suddenly free and he can't believe it either. He forgets whatever the play he was supposed to run is and goes up for what looks like an easy shot, except he doesn't have a shot because Alvin is suddenly there hovering above him. Alvin swats the ball away with a superhuman effort and then crashes down to the court. Jerry has gotten back up, grabs the ball and starts off down the court. Five Celtics are chasing him with six seconds left. Alvin is sitting there in a stupor watching Jerry running with the ball all alone.

Five, four, three, Jerry leaves the ground twenty feet from the hoop on the right side, two Celtics take off with him. One of them is six foot nine, the other is six foot five. Jerry is surrounded in midair, floating towards the basket. Two, they can't foul him or he'll make the free throw and win. Jerry doesn't miss free throws. They must cleanly block his shot. Jerry twists one way, appears to be about to shoot, then keeps the ball and as he's falling back to the court he swings the ball down, gripping it with both hands and flips it up towards the basket underhand between the two defenders. One, the ball arches above the hoop. Zero. It goes in.

43

I went out to Versailles the other day. Took the Metro. Not modern like BART but very nice and cheap too. I love looking at the French people. They look right back at you. They're very open about being curious. Versailles really killed me. I'd just love to bring the guys over here to see it. There's no way to describe it with words. It's really pretty disgusting in a way, all that useless wealth, but it sure is something to see.

I've sent a few postcards to Max's, one to Jerry, and a couple short letters to Louise, but I'm trying to keep my mind here, not back there.

I'm renting a room in a really nice run-down old hotel, pretty cheap and clean. I get my breakfast here, Continental style. Everybody calls me *Monsieur*. It's great. It sure beats the Busy Bee Motel, even though it doesn't have a television. Television isn't very big over here. I think that's because they know how to relax without it.

I've been in Europe for three months now. Went to England and Scotland, then came back to Paris. I like Paris. I feel right at home here for some reason. I'm learning the language pretty fast, though my accent is terrible. The girls here are really something.

Anyway, I got a letter from Louise a couple days ago. She said the play was going beautifully but she couldn't wait to get over here. I miss her, but not as much as I thought I would. I thought I might get over here and be really depressed without her, but that didn't happen. I like it here too much to be depressed. I want her to be here, but it's not like I'm desperate for her or anything. She said the stage in Max's is done and they got the delicatessen refrigerator counter installed and Edith is just ecstatic. Jackson's wife is pregnant and Bert and Jackson just got done swimming the San Francisco Bay again. Max is fine, she says, about the same as always. Stinky and Claire broke up, now Wings has a girlfriend and Blue says he'll say what he has to say when he sees me in the flesh again.

And Jerry is apparently going to sign a three-year contract with the Warriors for some huge amount of money. Louise said Jerry's talking about getting married to some dancer friend of Ellen's. That just floored me. I have the feeling, knowing Jerry, that he's going a little too fast as usual, but I'm happy he's in love. I just hope this woman is the right one for him. I mean, she's undoubtedly beautiful and intelligent, I just hope she isn't too crazy.

Louise says he told her he wants me to be the best man at his wedding. That's probably a stall tactic, since he knows I'm not coming home for a while.

Or maybe he really can't do it without me.